U0035175

NEW GEPT

新制全民英檢
中級 口說測驗
必考題型

陳頎／著
國際語言中心委員會／監修

全書MP3一次下載

9789864541799.zip

此為ZIP壓縮檔，iOS系統請升級至iOS 13以上再行下載，
其他系統請先安裝解壓縮程式或APP。
此為大型檔案（約140MB），建議使用WIFI連線下載，
以免占用流量，並確認連線狀況，以利下載順暢。

目 錄
CONTENTS

Chapter 1 實力養成

Chapter 2　考題透視

Part 3　看圖敘述 …………………………………… 223

Chapter 3　模擬試題

Chapter 1
實力養成

Part 1
考題介紹與
拿分致勝關鍵

學習目標

1. 了解英檢口說測驗的大概情況。

2. 學會在應試的時候應做什麼樣的準備。

3. 學會各種考試題型的基本破題技巧。

全民英檢中級口說能力測驗考題介紹與拿分致勝關鍵

一、全民英檢中級口說能力測驗考題介紹

全民英檢的中級口說測驗分為「朗讀短文」、「回答問題」與「看圖敘述」共三個部分。口說測驗的目的在測驗考生的口語表達以及聽懂題意的能力，因此，包括發音是否標準、語調是否流暢、回答是否符合題目要求、字彙片語的多寡都是重點。

「全民英檢中級口說」第一部分「朗讀短文」的重點是測試應考者發音與語調的正確性，朗讀的節奏也會顯現出對於句型的了解、文章意義的掌握程度。

第二部分是「回答問題」，共有 10 題。答題重點在於完全理解耳機傳來的問題，並且明確表達自己的想法。所以這個部分需要「聽說並重」，不能「答非所問」，也不能「不知所云」。題目包括 YES-NO 問句和疑問詞（WHAT, WHERE, HOW 等）問句，考生對於這兩種題目都必須完全熟悉。

第三部分「看圖敘述」是測驗考生能否正確描述圖片的內容。在這個部分有一張照片，以及三個引導作答的問題，考生需要根據提示進行 1 分 30 秒的敘述。這個部分的重點在於看清楚圖片，並且依照三個問題的重點進行描述。如果能多記一些常用

的地方副詞（例如 on the left of the picture 在照片的左邊，on the right of the picture 在照片的右邊，above 在上方，below 在下方，near 在附近，next to 在旁邊），以及關於形狀、大小、自然景物（例如 sky, ground, grass, trees, birds, animals）的詞彙，作答就會更順利。另外，回答時通常會用現在進行式（be + Ving）表達圖中人物的動作，以及用「There is / are...」的句型表達在場的人事物。

● 二、應試前的準備

1. 及早到場排隊：

　　口說能力測驗在語言教室舉行，建議各位考生早點到場，確認自己的教室，免得到時候時間不夠，不但要跟別的考生擠著確認自己在哪間教室應考，萬一遇到突發狀況（例如臨時換教室），也沒有足夠的時間應對。

2. 切換英文思考：

　　有些人在考試之前，會用中文聊天，這樣的行為其實會影響考試的表現。在說中文一段時間之後，忽然要轉換成用英文聽、說，就算是英文能力很好的人也會一時腦筋轉不過來。所以，如果有英文不錯的朋友陪考的話，請用英文聊天。沒有的話，也可以聽英文廣播或英文學習書的音檔。（不建議聽英文歌，因為歌曲的旋律和說話的語調完全不同），以保持大腦的英文反射思考環境。

3. 除了證件以外，其他東西可以不要帶就不要帶：

　　在參加考試時，如果帶了太多不必要的東西，反而容易影響應考的心情。在口說測驗時，連考試號碼也是用說的，這表示甚至連筆都不用帶。如果在考試前想做點別

的事情，聽英文音檔可以創造英文思考的環境，是比較好的選擇。

4. 確認錄音設備：

在正式考試前，考務人員會要求考生檢查設備，這時候一定要仔細檢查耳機、錄音機是否都運作正常。如果因為裝置故障而影響考試成績，就太冤枉了。

5. 放鬆心情，自然回答：

全民英檢口說測驗是在語言教室進行，與一般考試的教室不同，所以心情要放輕鬆，不要因為換了環境就覺得緊張、不適應。題目會透過耳機播放，回答時只要當成有人在你面前，自然說出口就行了。由於回答有時間限制，所以時間一到就必須停止作答，如果還繼續說下去，會讓自己聽不清楚下一個題目，而影響接下來的表現。而且，沒有說完整個句子並不是扣分的原因，所以不用為此感到擔心。

● 三、中級口說測驗各題型拿分致勝關鍵

第一部份　朗讀短文：

「朗讀短文」部分，主要是要了解應試者對發音、語調的掌握能力，應試者必須正確且自然地唸出短文。在朗讀短文之前，有一分鐘的時間可以先閱讀，應試者應該先了解文章的意義與目的，並揣摩作者的心境，以求朗讀時掌握正確的語調，唸起來便不會平淡而索然無味。在閱讀的時候，可以先默唸比較難的單字或發音，在正式朗讀時才不會慌亂。接下來兩分鐘的朗讀時間，則以正常的速度唸出。這個部分會有兩段不同的短文，字數各 80 字左右。文章內容大多與一般生活情境相關。

致勝關鍵 KeyPoints

1. 遇到不會唸的單字時，可用「自然發音」及「音節發音」單元所教的技巧唸出，儘量爭取分數，絕對不要跳過不唸。

2. 注意句子的語調變化，切忌逐字分別朗讀或語調無高低起伏，可用本書的「語調練習」及「句型練習」單元來加強語調的表現。

3. 若能兼顧發音的正確性，可達加分效果，但不必刻意強調，反而造成朗讀負擔。本書的「相似音比較」可提高您發音的準確度。

第二部分　回答問題：

　　此部分共有 10 題，前五題每題有 15 秒的回答時間，後五題則有 30 秒的回答時間，題目不在試題紙上，而是用聽的。因此，要答對題目的第一步就是要聽懂題目。前五題的題目比較簡單，後五題則需要多花一些時間說明理由，或者針對某個情境提出建議或提出問題。一般而言，15 秒的回答大約 3-4 句，30 秒的回答大約 5-6 句，但無論如何，都建議一直講到時間結束為止。時間結束後，一定要停止作答，以免錯過回答下一題的機會。

致勝關鍵 KeyPoints

1. 注意聽發問者的問題，尤其是開頭的疑問詞。熟讀本書「回答問題」模擬考題的「常見問句句型」，可增進「聽」問題的能力。

2. 小心「相似發音」導致「會錯意」、「答錯題目」，造成一分都拿不到的遺憾。

多加練習「相似音比較」，可以避免這樣的狀況。

3. 與寫作相同，在回答問題時，應該採用自己最有把握的句型，不要因為想拿高分而勉強使用自己不熟悉的進階文法。用錯了文法，不但不能提高分數，反而會因為犯錯而被扣分。詳讀「回答問題」各單元的「常見回答句型」，應付考試應該就綽綽有餘了。

第三部分　看圖敘述：

　　這個部分會有一張照片，以及三個引導作答的問題（最後一項則是請考生用剩餘的時間詳細描述圖片內容）。考生有 30 秒的時間可以看照片和題目，然後要用 1 分 30 秒的時間描述照片。回答時不要重述問題，只要直接進行敘述即可。問題通常是「這是什麼地方？」、「照片中的人在做什麼？」，以及要求推測圖中行為的目的、人物的態度、說話的內容等等。

致勝關鍵 KeyPoints

1. 必須回答題目所詢問的事項。這部分並不是「自由描述」，而是要以提示的問題作為回答的主軸。如果只是想到什麼就講什麼，而忘了談到題目所問的重點，也無法獲得高分。

2. 儘量完全利用一分半鐘的時間，徹底表現自己的敘述能力。如果真的沒有什麼好說，可以利用「看圖敘述」各單元的「必殺萬用句」來延長自己的說話內容。

Chapter 1
實力養成

Part 2
發音練習

學習目標

1. 學會自然發音，達成看到字母就會唸的目標。

2. 了解音節發音，遇到長的單字也不怕。

3. 分辨相似音，不怕聽題目的時候聽錯，也不怕講答案的時候講錯。

PART 2

發音重點
1

自然發音 (Phonics)

大部分的英文單字都可以依照拼字來推測發音。英語是以 a、e、i、o、u 等字母所代表的母音為核心，和其他字母所代表的子音結合，形成各種音節。下表依字母順序列出各種拼字可能的發音，遇到不會唸的單字時，可以依照這些規律推測發音。

0-00.mp3

A	a	[æ]	bag	van	brand
	a-e	[e]	lake	male	tame
	ai		chain	gain	jail
	ay		play	lay	ray
	al	[ɔ]	all	talk	walk
	aw		paw	law	saw
	au		haunt	cause	pause
	ar	[ɑr]	car	shark	mark
	air	[ɛr]	air	hair	fair
	are		dare	care	rare
B	b	[b]	boy	bite	lab
C	c	[s]	ice	race	pronounce
		[k]	care	came	clock
	ch	[tʃ]	church	check	watch
		[k]	school	stomach	Michael

發音練習

D	d	[d]	door	day	bed
E	e	[ɛ]	let	elephant	guest
	ea		meat	heat	bean
	ee	[i]	jeep	sheet	cheek
	e-e		Steve	theme	these
	er	[ɝ]	term	her	verb
	ear	[ɛr]	pear	tear	bear
		[ɪr]	tear	fear	hear
	eer	[ɪr]	beer	peer	deer
F	f	[f]	five	fish	life
G	g	[dʒ]	gym	gem	page
		[g]	good	god	dog
H	h	[h]	home	hair	horse
I	i	[ɪ]	mix	trip	split
	ie		pie	die	lie
	i-e	[aɪ]	vile	file	ice
	igh		high	thigh	night
	ir	[ɝ]	bird	first	shirt
J	j	[dʒ]	job	jam	juice
K	k	[k]	key	kind	week
L	l	[l]	loose	live	love
		[l]	soul	nail	bill
M	m	[m]	meet	mail	mall
		[m]	team	room	from
N	n	[n]	name	nose	nurse
		[n]	son	fun	noun
		[ŋ]	bank	think	link
	ng	[ŋ]	sing	thing	ring

O	o	[ɑ]	rob	slob	snob
	oa		goal	foam	loan
	oe	[o]	toe	Joe	foe
	o-e		bone	rope	spoke
	oo	[u]	boot	food	cool
		[ʊ]	took	cook	hook
	ou	[aʊ]	shout	found	mouse
	ow		bow	cow	vow
	oi	[ɔɪ]	oil	soil	coin
	oy		boy	toy	joy
	or	[ɔr]	form	tore	morning
P	p	[p]	pie	pink	stop
Q	qu	[kw]	queen	quick	quake
R	r	[r]	red	read	star
S	s	[s]	see	sit	bus
		[z]	rose	close	advise
	sh	[ʃ]	sheep	short	fish
T	t	[t]	tie	time	cut
	th	[θ]	three	thick	mouth
		[ð]	these	them	this
U	u	[ʌ]	gum	gun	jug
	ue	[u]	Sue	rue	true
	u-e	[ju]	tune	mute	cute
	ur	[ɝ]	burn	hurt	curse
V	v	[v]	vegetable	vet	have
W	w	[w]	way	wear	war
	wh	[hw]	where	when	what
X	x	[ks]	box	fax	fix
Y	y	[j]	yes	young	yo-yo
Z	z	[z]	zoo	size	jazz

發音重點
2

音節發音 (Syllables)

以下列舉單音節、兩個音節、三個音節、四個音節、五個音節的字來做練習。

一、單音節的單字 (Words of one syllable)

0-01.mp3

1. calm   calm   [kɑm]   冷靜的
    After several glasses of brandy, she felt **calm** again.

2. jet   jet   [dʒɛt]   噴射機
    I cannot fly a **jet** fighter.

3. John   John   [dʒɑn]   約翰
    My name is **John**. What's your name?

4. four   four   [for]   四
    There are **four** people in my family.

5. come   come   [kʌm]   來
    Please **come** in!

二、兩個音節的單字 (Words of two syllables)

0-02.mp3

1. ap·prove   approve   [ə`pruv]   贊同
    Do you **approve** of his decision?

2. bet·ter   better   [`bɛtɚ]   比較好的
Listen! I have a **better** idea!

3. broth·er   brother   [`brʌðɚ]   兄弟
Do you have any **brothers** or sisters?

4. cor·rect   correct   [kə`rɛkt]   正確
The answer is **correct**.

5. com·plain   complain   [kəm`plen]   抱怨
Don't **complain** to me. It wasn't my fault!

6. con·firm   confirm   [kən`fɜm]   確認
We're just calling you to **confirm** the date of your visit.

7. dan·ger   danger   [`dendʒɚ]   危險
Many children are in **danger** of domestic violence.

8. dis·cuss   discuss   [dɪ`skʌs]   討論
We still have some problems to **discuss**.

9. ma·jor   major   [`medʒɚ]   主要的
What is the **major** event in your life?

10. na·tion   nation   [`neʃən]   國家
The UK is the first industrial **nation** in the world.

11. pa·tient   patient   [`peʃənt]   病患
The **patient** should be separated from the others.

12. pres·sure   pressure   [`prɛʃɚ]   壓力
This apparatus is for measuring air **pressure**.

13. ques·tion   question   [`kwɛstʃən]   問題
I have a **question**.

14. re·quest   request   [rɪ`kwɛst]   請求
My parents turned a deaf ear to my **requests**.

15. sys·tem   system   [`sɪstəm]   制度
What is the education **system** like in Taiwan?

三、三個音節字 (Words of three syllables)

0-03.mp3

1. ac·ci·dent   accident   [`æksədənt]   意外事故
Mr. Green has become my neighbor after that **accident**.

2. ad·ven·ture   adventure   [əd`vɛntʃɚ]   冒險
I'm looking for some exciting **adventure**.

3. ap·point·ment   appointment   [ə`pɔɪntmənt]   約定的會面
I have an **appointment** with Dr. Lee.

4. at·ti·tude   attitude   [`ætətjud]   態度
Does she have a good **attitude** at school?

5. chem·is·try   chemistry   [`kɛmɪstrɪ]   化學
I'm going to study **chemistry** in the university.

6. con·cen·trate   concentrate   [`kɑnsɛnˌtret]   專注
Keep quiet! I can't **concentrate** at all!

7. en·er·gy   energy   [`ɛnɚˌdʒɪ]   精力
I have run out of **energy**.

8. em·pha·sis   emphasis   [`ɛmfəsɪs]   強調
Many parents put great **emphasis** on children's school marks.

9. in·flu·ence   influence   [`ɪnflʊəns]   影響
The story has **influenced** a lot of people.

10. par·a·graph   paragraph   [`pærə͵græf]   段落
How many **paragraphs** are in the article?

11. pop·u·lar   popular   [`pɑpjələ˞]   流行的
Baseball is very **popular** in Taiwan.

12. re·cep·tion   reception   [rɪ`sɛpʃən]   接待
Thank you for your **reception**.

13. sat·is·fy   satisfy   [`sætɪs͵faɪ]   使滿足
I'm sure the result will **satisfy** you.

14. Sep·tem·ber   September   [sɛp`tɛmbə˞]   九月
We will start the next semester in **September**.

15. um·brel·la   umbrella   [ʌm`brɛlə]   雨傘
Don't forget to bring your **umbrella**.

四、四個音節的單字 (Words of four syllables)

0-04.mp3

1. dec·o·ra·tion   decoration   [͵dɛkə`reʃən]   裝飾
I don't like a house with too much **decoration**.

2. dic·tion·a·ry   dictionary   [`dɪkʃən͵ɛrɪ]   字典
Please look up the word in the **dictionary**.

3. dif·fi·cul·ty   difficulty   [ˈdɪfəˌkʌltɪ]   困難
I can use English without any **difficulties**.

4. el·e·va·tor   elevator   [ˈɛləˌvetɚ]   電梯
The **elevator** will stop on the seventh floor.

5. gen·er·al·ly   generally   [ˈdʒɛnərəlɪ]   通常
Generally speaking, it isn't really difficult to use English.

6. hy·poth·e·sis   hypothesis   [haɪˈpɑθəsɪs]   假設
That's an interesting **hypothesis**, but is there any evidence?

7. in·vi·ta·tion   invitation   [ˌɪnvəˈteʃən]   邀請
I have sent her my **invitation**.

8. Jan·u·ar·y   January   [ˈdʒænjʊˌɛrɪ]   一月
January is the first month of the year.

9. my·thol·o·gy   mythology   [mɪˈθɑlədʒɪ]   神話
Dragons exist in Chinese **mythology**.

10. ob·ser·va·tion   observation   [ˌɑbzɚˈveʃən]   觀察
The report is based on my **observation**.

11. pho·tog·ra·phy   photography   [fəˈtɑgrəfɪ]   攝影術
Do you have an eye for **photography**?

12. psy·chol·o·gy   psychology   [saɪˈkɑlədʒɪ]   心理學
Psychology is a very interesting subject.

13. re·con·struc·tion   reconstruction   [ˌrikənˈstrʌkʃən]   重建
The **reconstruction** of this building has just completed.

14. re·cov·er·y   recovery   [rɪ`kʌvərɪ]   復元
He should stay here for his **recovery**.

15. sat·is·fac·tion   satisfaction   [ˌsætɪs`fækʃən]   滿足
They left with **satisfaction**.

五、五個音節字 (Words of five syllables)

0-05.mp3

1. in·stru·men·ta·tion instrumentation   [ˌɪnstrəmen`teʃən]   儀表，儀器
The car's **instrumentation** is old.

2. hes·i·ta·ting·ly   hesitatingly   [`hɛzəˌtetɪŋlɪ]   言語支吾地
He spoke **hesitatingly** with a low voice.

3. or·di·nar·i·ly   ordinarily   [`ɔrdṇˌɛrɪlɪ]   平常地
Ordinarily, the bus will come by 10 o'clock.

4. mi·li·tar·i·ly   militarily   [`mɪləˌtɛrɪlɪ]   在軍事上
Malaysia and Indonesia are not **militarily** friendly with Singapore.

5. ap·prox·i·mate·ly approximately   [ə`prɑksəmɪtlɪ]   大概；近乎
It is **approximately** 12:30.

6. con·tem·po·rar·y   contemporary   [kən`tɛmpəˌrɛrɪ]   同時代的
We aren't **contemporary** with Jesus Christ.

7. in·hos·pit·a·ble   inhospitable   [ɪn`hɑspɪtəb]]   不親切的
The old man is very **inhospitable**.

8. syn·thet·i·cal·ly   synthetically   [sɪn`θɛtɪklɪ]   以合成方式
The factory manufactures the products **synthetically**.

9. an·ni·ver·sa·ry   anniversary   [ˌænə`vɝsərɪ]   週年
Next week will be my grandparents' 40th wedding **anniversary**.

10. al·pha·be·ti·cal   alphabetical   [ˌælfə`bɛtɪkl]   依字母順序的
Almost all dictionaries are **alphabetical**.

11. op·por·tu·ni·ty   opportunity   [ˌɑpə`tjunətɪ]   機會
It's a great **opportunity** to work here.

12. caf·e·te·ri·a   cafeteria   [ˌkæfə`tɪrɪə]   自助餐廳
There are nice **cafeterias** on each side of this alley.

13. u·ni·ver·si·ty   university   [ˌjunə`vɝsətɪ]   大學
Have you graduated from the **university**?

14. rec·om·men·da·tion   recommendation   [ˌrɛkəmɛn`deʃən]   推薦
I would appreciate a letter of **recommendation**.

15. or·gan·i·za·tion   organization   [ˌɔrgənə`zeʃən]   組織
Government is a big **organization**.

PART 2

發音重點
3

相似音比較 (Distinguish similar pronunciations)

以下列舉多組相似音的例子來做比較。

1 [i] / [ɪ]

0-06.mp3

[i]	[ɪ]
peel	pill
heel	hill

peel 脫皮;剝（水果、蔬菜）皮 / pill 藥丸

1. My face began to **peel** from the sunburn I had last time on the beach.

   我的臉從我上次在海灘上曬傷的地方開始脫皮了。

2. Jason usually has to take the sleeping **pill** before sleep.

   Jason 通常得在睡前吃安眠藥。

heel 腳後跟;鞋跟 / hill 小山丘

1. The **heels** of this pair of shoes were just too high for me.

   這雙鞋的鞋跟對我來說太高了。

2. They made a great effort to climb up the **hill**.

   他們做了很大的努力爬上山丘。

② [e] / [ɛ] / [æ]

0-07.mp3

[e]	[ɛ]	[æ]
train	ten	tan
pain	pen	pan
main	men	man

train 火車 / ten 十 / tan 棕褐色；曬成棕褐色的皮膚

1. What time does the **train** come?　火車幾點來？
2. Do you have **ten** dollars?　你有十塊錢嗎？
3. Come to look at the **tan** on my arm.
   來看我手臂上被曬成棕褐色的皮膚。

pain 疼痛 / pen 筆 / pan 平底鍋

1. I feel **pain** in my right leg.　我右腿感覺到疼痛。
2. May I borrow your **pen**?　我可以跟你借筆嗎？
3. Fry an egg in the **pan**.　在平底鍋裡面炒一個蛋。

main 主要的 / men 男人（複數）/ man 男人（單數）

1. I can't see the **main** point of the article.　我看不出這篇文章的重點。
2. C'mon, let's fight like **men**!　來吧，像男子漢一樣決鬥吧！
3. John is a **man**'s name.　John 是男人的名字。

3 [ɑ] / [ʌ]

0-08.mp3

[ɑ]	[ʌ]
lock	luck
collar	color

lock 鎖 / luck 運氣

1. Make sure the door is **locked** before leaving.
   離開前要確定門是鎖上的。
2. The hotel was full, so we decided to try our **luck** elsewhere.
   那間旅館客滿了，所以我們決定到其他地方去碰碰運氣。

collar 領子 / color 顏色

1. What size of **collar** is this shirt?　這件襯衫的領子是什麼尺寸？
2. What **color** did you paint the door?　你把門漆成什麼顏色？

4 [ɑ] / [aʊ]

0-09.mp3

[ɑ]	[aʊ]
shot	shout
pond	pound

shot 射擊、射門、投籃 / shout 大喊

1. It's another good **shot** from Michael Jordan.
   麥可・喬丹另一個漂亮的投籃。

2. The football fans are **shouting** their team name.

足球迷正在大喊著他們的隊名。

---

pond 池塘 / pound 磅；英鎊

1. There is a small **pond** in the garden.　在這個花園裡有一座小池塘。

2. 1 **pound** is approximately equal to 0.45 kilograms.

一磅差不多相當於 0.45 公斤。

5 [o] / [ɔ]

0-10.mp3

[o]	[ɔ]
coast	cost
low	law

---

coast 海岸 / cost 價值、價錢、花費

1. People living on the south **coast** in the U.S. enjoy more sunshine in the winter than people living in Canada.

在冬天，住在美國南方海岸的人享受比住在加拿大的人更多的陽光。

2. The **cost** of buying this LV bag was more than I'd expected.

買這個 LV 皮包的花費比我想像的還多。

---

low 低 / law 法律、法令

1. They spoke in **low** voices so I would not hear what they were saying.

他們用很低的聲音講話，讓我聽不到他們在說什麼。

2. There are **laws** against drinking in the street.

有禁止在街上飲酒的法令。

6 [ɔ] / [ɝ]

0-11.mp3

[ɔ]	[ɝ]
walk	work
cause	curse

walk 走路、散步 / work 工作

1. I like to take a **walk** after dinner. 　我喜歡在晚餐後去散步。
2. Sorry, I can't go with you. I have **work** tonight.
   抱歉，我不能跟你去。我今晚有工作。

cause 導致 / curse 詛咒

1. Deforestation will **cause** many disasters.
   森林破壞將導致許多的災難。
2. The wizards tried to **curse** the hero. 　男巫們試著去詛咒這位英雄。

7 [u] / [ʊ]

0-12.mp3

[u]	[ʊ]
food	foot
tool	took

food 食物 / foot 腳

1. What kind of **food** do you like most? 　你最喜歡什麼樣的食物？
2. He took off the sock from his right **foot**. 　他從他的右腳脫下襪子。

tool 工具 / took 取走、拿走（take 的過去式）

1. The best **tool** for you to study English is an English dictionary.

   對你而言，學習英文最好的工具就是一本英文字典。

2. A thief **took** my wallet away yesterday.　昨天一個賊拿走了我的皮包。

8 [ɔ] / [ɔɪ]

0-13.mp3

[ɔ]	[ɔɪ]
all	oil
bald	boil

all 全部 / oil 油

1. **All** my brothers are married.　我所有的兄弟們都結婚了。

2. The face **oil** can keep the water in your skin.

   這罐臉部保養油可以把水分保持在你的皮膚裡。

bald 光頭的 / boil 煮沸

1. I saw the thief was **bald**.　我看到那個小偷是光頭。

2. It's better to drink **boiled** water.　喝煮沸過的水比較好。

9 [b] / [p]

0-14.mp3

[b]	[p]
cab	cup
robe	rope

cab 計程車 / cup （一）杯；獎盃

1. We took the **cab** to get to the Taipei Railway Station.

   我們搭計程車去台北火車站。

2. The **cup** by the TV got knocked over by someone yesterday.

   昨天電視旁的杯子被人打翻了。

robe 外袍 / rope 繩子

1. The judge put on his **robe** and called her into an empty courtroom.

   法官穿上他的外袍並且叫她進入空蕩蕩的法庭。

2. He tied the stone with thick **rope**.

   他用粗的繩子把石頭綁起來。

⑩ [k] / [g]

0-15.mp3

[k]	[g]
back	bag
coat	goat

back 回來 / bag 袋子

1. When will you be **back**?　你何時將回來？

2. Could you give me three **bags**?　你可以給我三個袋子嗎？

coat 大衣 / goat 山羊

1. The old man took off his **coat** when he came into the room.

   當那個老男人進到房間時，他把他的大衣脫下來。

2. Do you know the differences between sheep and **goats**?

你知道綿羊和山羊的不同嗎？

11 [l] / [r]

0-16.mp3

[l]	[r]
pool	poor
liver	river

pool 池 / poor 窮困的

1. I go to a swimming **pool** once a week.　我每個禮拜去一次游泳池。
2. He is a **poor** man.　他是一個窮困的男人。

liver 肝 / river 河

1. 20% of people infected with hepatitis B virus will develop **liver** cancer.　20% 罹患 B 型肝炎病毒的人會發展成肝癌。
2. There is a **river** in front of my house.　我家前面有一條河。

12 [f] / [v]

0-17.mp3

[f]	[v]
leaf	leave
face	vase

leaf 葉子 / leave 離開

1. I wrote her name on a **leaf**. 我把她的名字寫在葉子上。

2. Tom's recently decided to **leave** Paris for New York.

   Tom 最近決定要離開巴黎去紐約。

face 臉 / vase 花瓶

1. Mary has a round **face**. 瑪莉有一張圓臉。

2. My nephew broke the **vase** this morning.

   我姪子今天早上把花瓶打破了。

⓭ [s] / [z]

0-18.mp3

[s]	[z]
advice	advise
race	raise

advice 建議，勸告（名詞）/ advise 建議，勸告（動詞）

1. Acting on her **advice**, Tom decided to give up smoking.

   為了實現她的勸告，湯姆決定戒菸。

2. Maria **advised** her colleague to take the MRT to work to save time.

   瑪莉亞建議她的同事搭捷運上班以節省時間。

race 賽跑，競速比賽 / raise 舉起

1. Will you run a **race** at the annual field day?

   你會在年度運動會上參加賽跑嗎？

2. **Raise** your hand if you have any questions.

如果你有任何問題就舉起你的手。

⑭ [s] / [θ]

0-19.mp3

[s]	[θ]
mouse	mouth
sink	think

mouse 老鼠 / mouth 嘴巴

1. I saw a big **mouse** in the kitchen last night.

我昨晚在廚房看到一隻大老鼠。

2. Don't let her know about this. She has a big **month**.

不要讓她知道這件事。她是個大嘴巴。

sink 下沉 / think 思考，想

1. Help! The boat is **sinking**. 救命啊！這艘船在下沉。

2. Keep quiet! I'm **thinking** about how to solve the problem!

安靜！我在思考如何解決這個問題。

⑮ [z] / [θ]

0-20.mp3

[z]	[θ]
close	cloth
nose	north

close 關上 / cloth 布

1. Would you mind if I **close** the window?

   如果我關上窗戶，你會介意嗎？

2. The **cloth** is too small for me.　對我來說這塊布太小了。

nose 鼻子 / north 北部

1. You should use your **nose** to pronounce the letter "N".

   你應該用你的鼻子來發「N」這個字母。

2. I live in the **north** of Taipei.　我住在台北的北部。

⑯ [θ] / [ð]

0-21.mp3

[θ]	[ð]
breath	breathe
bath	bathe

breath 呼吸（名詞）/ breathe 呼吸（動詞）

1. She took a deep **breath** before signing the document.

   她在簽文件之前深深吸了一口氣。

2. He needs a life-support machine to keep **breathing**.

   他需要生命維持系統來保持呼吸。

bath （洗）澡（名詞）/ bathe 洗澡（動詞）

1. I'm going to take a **bath**.　我要去洗個澡了。

2. Isn't it tough to **bathe** a dog?　幫狗洗澡不是一件很難的事嗎？

 **[ʃ] / [ʒ]**

0-22.mp3

[ʃ]	[ʒ]
pressure	pleasure
mission	vision

pressure 壓力 / pleasure 榮幸

1. I think being an editor is a high-**pressure** job.
   我認為當編輯是一個壓力很大的工作。
2. May I have the **pleasure** to dance with you?
   我有這個榮幸跟您跳支舞嗎?

mission 任務 / vision 願景

1. What is the **mission** this time?　這次的任務是什麼?
2. To keep developing the market in China is the **vision** of our company.
   持續發展在中國的市場是我們公司的願景。

 **[ʃ] / [tʃ]**

0-23.mp3

[ʃ]	[tʃ]
wash	watch
cash	catch

wash 洗 / watch 錶

1. I **wash** my hair every day.　我每天洗我的頭髮。

2. My father gave me a **watch** for my birthday.

   我父親給我一只錶當生日禮物。

cash 現金 / catch 捉，拿，接

1. We only accept **cash** and checks.　我們只收現金跟支票。

2. The left fielder ran very fast to **catch** the ball.

   左外野手跑得非常快去接球。

⑲ [tʃ] / [dʒ]

0-24.mp3

[tʃ]	[dʒ]
lunch	lunge
chain	Jane

lunch 午餐 / lunge 突刺

1. Have you had **lunch** yet?　你吃了午餐嗎？

2. The knight **lunged** his spear into the dragon's heart.

   騎士將他的長槍突刺進龍的心臟。

chain 鎖鏈 / Jane（女性名）

1. The **chain** broke and the door remained open.

   鎖鏈壞了，而門保持開著的狀態。

2. **Jane** has long beautiful dark hair.　珍有一頭長而且美麗的黑色頭髮。

0-25.mp3

⑳ [m] / [n]

[m]	[n]
mail	nail
map	nap
some	son
gum	gun

mail 郵寄 / nail 釘子

1. Please send the application form by **mail**.
   請用郵寄的方式寄送申請表。

2. This museum was built without any **nails**.
   這座博物館不用任何釘子建造。

map 地圖 / nap 小睡

1. Where are we on the **map**? 我們在地圖的哪裡？

2. We usually take a **nap** after lunch. 我們經常在午餐後小睡一下。

some 一些 / son 兒子

1. I have **some** good news for you. 我有一些好消息要告訴你。

2. My oldest **son** lives in Paris. 我最大的兒子住在巴黎。

gum 口香糖 / gun 槍

1. Do not eat, drink or chew **gum** in the train.
   不要在列車內飲食及嚼口香糖。

2. The burglar fired the **gun** when he was running away.

小偷在逃走時開了槍。

㉑ [n] / [ŋ]

0-26.mp3

[n]	[ŋ]
ran	rang
sin	sing

ran 跑（run 的過去式）/ rang 響（ring 的過去式）

1. He **ran** for 5,000 meters yesterday.　他昨天跑了五千公尺。

2. The phone **rang** when I was taking a shower.

當我在洗澡的時候，電話響了。

sin 罪孽 / sing 唱歌

1. You should repent from your **sins**.　你應該從你的罪孽中悔改。

2. Would you like to **sing** with me?　你想要跟我一起唱歌嗎？

Chapter 1
實力養成

Part 3
語調練習

學習目標

1. 熟悉英文的自然會話腔調，以增進自己的英文聽力。

2. 跟著外籍老師複誦，學習最道地的英文腔調及感情表達。

PART 3

類型 1

降調 (Falling intonation)

說明：英語的降調表示肯定、平和、穩定的情緒，通常用於直述句、祈使句及 wh- 問句。

一、直述句（Declarative sentences）

0-27.mp3

例句：

You have a car.

You can go now.

其他例句：

1) The sun is shining.　太陽閃耀著。

2) The birds are singing.　鳥兒歌唱著。

3) I am fine.　我很好。

4) He gave me a ride yesterday.　他昨天載我一程。

5) She has been to Canada.　她曾經去過加拿大。

6) You are right.　你是對的。

7) My father and I had a long discussion last night.

昨天晚上我父親跟我進行了很長時間的討論。

8) It sounds like you already knew it.　聽起來好像你已經知道這件事了。

9) I would like to have an appointment with my doctor.

我想跟我的醫生安排會面（看診）。

10) I wonder if you would like to visit uncle Lee.

我想知道你是否想拜訪李叔叔。

0-28.mp3

● 二、祈使句（Imperative sentences）

例句：

Come here.

Leave me alone.

其他例句：

1) Stop chasing me!　停止追我！

2) Push the button!　按下這個按鈕！

3) Open the door!　打開門！

4) Repeat after me!　跟著我複誦！

5) Behave yourself!　注意你的行為舉止！

6) Don't think too much. It will be fine.　別想太多，會沒事的。

7) Don't worry about me.　不要擔心我。

8) Please, take a seat and have something to drink by yourself.

請坐，並請自己拿飲料。

9) Let's go to see a movie together.　我們一起去看電影吧。

10) Be sensible!　理智點！

三、Wh- 問句（Wh-questions）

0-29.mp3

例句：

What is your name?

Who has been to China?

其他例句：

1) Who is the person standing over there?　站在那邊的那個人是誰？

2) Who is best for this job?　誰是做這個工作的最佳人選？

3) When will you be back?　你何時會回來？

4) When did she leave?　她什麼時候離開的？

5) Where did he go?　他去了哪裡？

6) Where is John's house?　約翰的房子在哪？

7) What's the matter with you?　你怎麼了？

8) What do you do for a living?　你做什麼工作？

9) How do you go to school every day?　你每天怎麼上學的？

10) Why is the sky blue?　為什麼天空是藍的？

類型 *2*

升調 (Rising intonation)

說明：英語的升調表示懷疑、不確定、驚訝的情緒，通常用於 Yes-No 問句及
附加問句。

● 一、YES-NO 問句（Yes-No Questions）

0-30.mp3

例句：

Will you call me tomorrow?

May I call you back later?

其他例句：

1) May I help you?　需要幫忙嗎？

2) Are you alright?　你還好嗎？

3) Should we start?　我們是不是該開始了？

4) Could you give me a hand?　你能幫我的忙嗎？

5) Aren't they beautiful?　它們不漂亮嗎？

6) Have you had dinner yet?　你晚餐吃了沒？

7) Must I stay?　我必須留下來嗎？

8) Am I not?　我不是嗎？

9) Do I know you? 我認識你嗎？

10) Is it true? 這是真的嗎？

二、附加問句（Tag Questions）

0-31.mp3

例句：

I didn't say that, did I?

You will come tomorrow, won't you?

其他例句：

1) He is a funny guy, isn't he? 他是個有趣的傢伙，不是嗎？

2) I am terrible, aren't I? 我很糟糕，不是嗎？

3) You don't believe them, do you? 你不相信他們，是嗎？

4) Mary doesn't have a car, does she? 瑪麗沒有車吧，有嗎？

5) She has a computer, doesn't she? 她有一台電腦，不是嗎？

6) He has never been to Australia, has he? 他從來沒去過澳洲吧，有嗎？

7) Let's go out for dinner, shall we? 我們一起出門吃晚餐，好嗎？

8) You will stay here, won't you? 你會待在這裡，不是嗎？

9) There are three people in your family, aren't there?
   你家有三個人，不是嗎？

10) Listen to me, will you? 聽我說話，好嗎？

類型 *3*

先升後降 (Rise-fall intonation)

● 一、否定句（Negative sentences）

0-32.mp3

例句：

I don't like fish.

You can't do that.

其他例句：

1) I'm not stupid.　我不笨。

2) You aren't reading a book.　你不是正在看書。

3) He isn't innocent.　他不是無辜的。

4) That can't be true.　那不可能是真的。

5) You shouldn't have done that!　你不應該做了那件事！

6) We haven't had any food.　我們還沒吃任何東西。

7) I won't say anything.　我不會說出任何事情。

8) There aren't any apples.　沒有任何蘋果。

9) You needn't leave.　你不必離開。

10) She didn't sleep last night.　她昨天晚上沒有睡覺。

二、選擇疑問句（Alternative questions）

0-33.mp3

例句：

Would you like tea or coffee?

Is it sunny or cloudy?

其他例句：

1) Which color do you like? Red or green?

    你喜歡哪個顏色？紅的或綠的？

2) Which answer is correct? A, B or C?

    哪個答案是正確的？ A，B 還是 C ？

3) Will he come on Saturday or on Sunday?

    他會在星期六還是星期天來？

4) Is this yours or mine?　這是你的還是我的？

5) What should I buy? Sugar or salt?　我應該買什麼？糖還是鹽？

6) Now then, should I turn to the right or to the left?

    好，現在，我該轉向右還是轉向左？

7) Where will you go? Post office or bank?　你要去哪裡？郵局還是銀行？

8) How do you come to school? By bus or on foot?

    你是怎麼來學校的？搭公車還是走路？

9) Is a banana red, pink or yellow?　香蕉是紅色、粉紅色還是黃色？

三、列舉單字或片語（Series of words or phrases）

例句：

The house has a big kitchen, a

bathroom, and a large living room.

0-34.mp3

其他例句：

1) She likes dogs, cats, and monkeys.　她喜歡狗、貓跟猴子。

2) There are three people in my family: Mom, Dad and me.

我家有三個人：我媽、我爸和我。

3) I took my umbrella, put on my shoes then left home.

我拿了我的雨傘，穿上我的鞋子，然後就離開家了。

4) He sent me a letter, a bunch of roses, and a ring.

他送來一封信、一束玫瑰及一只戒指給我。

5) I have been to 3 countries: the USA, Japan and New Zealand.

我曾經去過三個國家：美國、日本和紐西蘭。

6) Norman, Jason and I went to see a movie yesterday.

諾曼、傑森和我昨天去看一部電影。

Chapter 1
實力養成

Part 4
句型練習

學習目標

1. 了解 8 大類英文句型的發音重點。

2. 熟悉 8 大類英文句型及其語調,使自己在英檢口說測驗的「回答問題」、「看圖敘述」中,更能發揮得淋漓盡致。

PART 4

第 *1* 類

基本直述句 (Declarative sentences)

0-35.mp3 發音提示 粗體套色字為重音，加底線者為連音。

1 **Birds** fly **high**.

鳥高飛。

發音重點 bird 的 ir 發 [ɝ] 的重音並捲舌。

2 A **bird** is in the **tree**.

鳥在樹上。

發音重點 tree 中的 tr 發 [tr]，而 ee 則要發長音 [i]。

3 **Birds** fly to the **sky**.

鳥飛上天空。

發音重點 bird 的 ir 發 [ɝ] 的重音並捲舌。sky 中的 k 音不送氣。

4 A **bird** <u>flew across</u> the **park**.

鳥飛越公園。

發音重點 park 要有捲舌音。

- -

5 John **suddenly** fell off the **bicycle**.

約翰突然從腳踏車上摔下。

發音重點 suddenly 為副詞，修飾掉下來的動作，因此發音時可以特別

強調。

- -

6 I love my **family** so much.

我很愛我的家人。

發音重點 family 的 a 發 [æ] 音，要明顯。

- -

7 He loves his family **as well**.

他也愛他的家人。

發音重點 這句話表達的重點是他「同樣」愛家人，所以可以強調 as well。

- -

8 Mom gives me a **ride** to school.

媽媽載我去學校。

發音重點 ride 的 i 是雙母音 [aɪ]。

- -

9 I was **given a lift** to my workplace by my friend.

我讓我的朋友載到工作的地方。

發音重點　was given a lift 是被動態，為了強調這個行為，可以稍微大
聲一點。

10 Father **gave** Susan a **dictionary** as a **birthday gift**.

父親給蘇珊一本字典當作生日禮物。

發音重點　dictionary 的 ary 發 [ɛrɪ]，而 birthday 的 ir 要發 [ɚ] 的重音並
捲舌。

11 Susan was **given a dictionary** as a **birthday present** by Father.

蘇珊被父親給了一本字典當作生日禮物。

發音重點　發音時稍微強調被動態的動作部分。

12 A book was **given** to Sue as a **birthday gift**.

一本書被給了蘇當作生日禮物。

發音重點　發音時稍微強調被動態的動作部分。

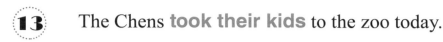

13 The Chens **took their kids** to the zoo today.

陳家人今天帶他們的小孩到動物園。

發音重點 take 的 a 發長音 [e]。

14 Mr. Brown **took his kitten** for a walk today.

伯朗先生今天帶他的小貓去散步。

發音重點 kitten 中的 i 發短音 [ɪ]。

15 The Browns' kids were **taken** to the zoo today.

伯朗家的小孩今天被帶到動物園。

發音重點 發音時稍微強調被動態的動作部分。

16 Mr. Chen's puppy was <u>brought along</u> with him for a walk.

陳先生的小狗被他一起帶去散步。

發音重點 發音時稍微強調被動態的動作部分,而 brought 的 ought 發音為 [ɔt],gh 不發音。

17 I **make it a rule** to **get up early** every day.

我規定自己每天早起。

發音重點　make it a rule 是立下規定的意思，稍微強調。

18 Brian has a **habit** of **getting up** early every day.

布萊恩有每天早起的習慣。

發音重點　habit 的 a 發 [æ] 的音，getting 要確實發出 ing 的 [ɪŋ] 音。

19 We usually like to **go shopping** on weekends.

我們通常喜歡在週末去購物。

發音重點　go shopping 是本句的重點，要稍微強調。

20 Tom usually likes to **go window shopping** on weekends.

湯姆通常喜歡在週末去逛街。

發音重點　go window shopping 是本句的重點，要稍微強調。

第 **2** 類

基本否定句 (Negative sentences)

0-36.mp3 發音提示 粗體套色字為重音，加底線者為連音。

1 I don't like this coffee **that much**.

我不是很喜歡這個咖啡。

發音重點 強調 that much。

2 He doesn't want to **stay in Taipei**.

他不想要待在台北。

發音重點 強調 stay in Taipei。

3 I am <u>ashamed</u> of not realizing it.

我對於不知此事感到羞愧。

發音重點 am ashamed of 是感到羞愧的意思，ashamed 的發音是

[ə`ʃemd]。

4 I have **little** money.

我只有一點錢。

發音重點 強調 little。

- -

5 There is **little hope** of his success.

他成功的希望很渺茫。

發音重點 強調 little hope。

- -

6 Mei has had **few friends ever since** she <u>was a</u> <u>student at school.</u>

梅自從是學校學生時就只有很少的朋友。

發音重點 本句強調 few friends，ever since 則是「自從」的意思。

- -

7 He <u>**can't afford**</u> to buy that car. **Neither** <u>can I.</u>

他無法負擔買那輛車。我也不能。

發音重點 can't afford 是無法負擔的意思，是需要強調的部分。neither 是「也不」的意思，也需要強調。

- -

8 Neither **David** nor **I** am right.

大衛與我都不對。

發音重點 強調 David 與 I 兩者皆非。

- -

9 He neither **drinks** nor **smokes**.

他不喝酒也不抽菸。

發音重點 強調既不 drinks 也不 smokes。

- -

10 Ted can read neither **English** nor **German**.

泰德既不會讀英文也不會讀德文。

發音重點 強調 English 與 German 都不會。

- -

11 Kevin didn't like **horror movies** in the past.

凱文以前不喜歡恐怖電影。

發音重點 horror movies 是恐怖電影的意思，也是句子要表達的主要內容，所以需要強調。horror 的發音是 [`hɔrɚ]。

- -

12 I **haven't been** to this place before.

我以前從來沒去過這個地方。

發音重點 強調 haven't been。

· ·

13 My income can **hardly** meet the month's cost.

我的收入很難應付這個月的支出。

發音重點 強調 hardly，表示很難。

· ·

14 There's **hardly** any time left.

幾乎沒剩下任何時間。

發音重點 強調 hardly，表示幾乎不。

· ·

第 3 類

基本疑問句 (Interrogative sentences)

0-37.mp3　發音提示　粗體套色字為重音，加底線者為連音。

1 Who will **come to the party** tomorrow?

明天誰會參加派對？

發音重點　強調 who 與 come to the party。

2 Who do you know has **seen that romance** before?

你知道有誰看過那部愛情電影嗎？

發音重點　強調 who 和 seen that romance。romance 的 ce 發音是 [s]。

3 Who is the girl **in the red dress** over there?

那邊那位穿著紅色洋裝的女孩是誰？

發音重點　強調 who 以及 in the red dress，其中 red 的 e 發音是 [ɛ]。

④ **Who** is willing to **cook dinner tonight**?

今晚誰願意煮晚餐？

發音重點 強調 who 以及 cook dinner tonight。

⑤ **Who's singing** in the KTV?

誰正在 KTV 唱歌？

發音重點 強調 who's singing。

⑥ **Who knows what's wrong** with her?

誰知道她怎麼了嗎？

發音重點 強調 who knows what's wrong。

⑦ **Where** is the **national museum** located?

國家博物館位於哪裡？

發音重點 強調 where 和 national museum。

⑧ **Where** is the **camera shop**?

相機店在哪裡？

發音重點 強調 where 和 camera shop。

What <u>did **I** do wrong</u>?

我做錯了什麼？

發音重點 強調 what 與 I do wrong。

- -

 Do you know **where we are now**?

你知道我們現在在哪裡嗎？

發音重點 強調 where we are now。

- -

 <u>Would you</u> be so kind to show us **where we are now**?

可以請您告知我們現在在哪裡嗎？

發音重點 強調 where we are now。

- -

 What color <u>is your</u> car?

你的車子是什麼顏色的？

發音重點 強調 what color。

- -

 What size do you want?

你要什麼尺寸？

發音重點 強調 what size。

- -

14 **What do you say** to taking a taxi?

你覺得搭計程車如何？

發音重點 強調 what do you say。

15 **Why** are you driving **by yourself**?

你為什麼自己一個人開車？

發音重點 強調 why 與 by yourself。

第 4 類

祈使句 (Imperative sentences)

0-38.mp3 發音提示 粗體套色字為重音,加底線者為連音。

1 **Be nice** to your friends!

對你的朋友好一些!

發音重點 強調 be nice。

2 **Be careful**!

小心點!

發音重點 強調 be careful。

3 <u>**Watch out**</u>!

小心!

發音重點 強調 watch out。

4 **Come in**, please.

請進。

發音重點 強調 come in。

5 **Keep the change**.

零錢留著（不用找了）。

發音重點 強調 keep the change。

6 **Keep off** the grass.

不准踏草皮。

發音重點 強調 keep off。

7 **Have a seat**.

請坐下。

發音重點 強調 have a seat。

8 **Put your cup** over here.

把你的杯子放在這裡。

發音重點 強調 put your cup。

9 **Drop me** at that corner.

在那個街角讓我下車。

發音重點 強調 drop me。

10 **Open the door** for me.

幫我開門。

發音重點 強調 open the door。

11 **Wait a minute**.

稍等一下。

發音重點 強調 wait a minute。

12 **Wait** till I return.

等我回來。

發音重點 強調 wait。

13 **Watch** your manners, young man.

年輕人，注意你的禮節。

發音重點 強調 watch。

14 **Have some tea**.

來點茶吧。

發音重點 強調 have some tea。

15 **Have some coffee**.

來點咖啡。

發音重點 強調 have some coffee。

16 **Drop me a line** <u>if you</u> need further information.

如果你需要更進一步的資訊,請寫信給我。

發音重點 強調 drop me a line,其中 drop 的 o 發 [ɑ] 的音。

17 **Tell him** what he did **wrong**.

告訴他哪裡做錯了。

發音重點 強調 tell him 與 wrong。

18 **Go to the** <u>post office</u> after you finish typing this letter.

你打完這封信後去郵局一趟。

發音重點 強調 go to the post office。

19 Please **give yourself** a chance.

請給自己一個機會。

發音重點 強調 give yourself。

 20 Please **let me go**.

請讓我走。

發音重點 強調 let me go。

第 5 類

因果句 (Cause-and-effect sentences)

0-39.mp3 發音提示 粗體套色字為重音，加底線者為連音。

---

1 <u>As a</u> result of the **police's requirements**, the man was **taken into the police station**.

因為警方的要求，那個男人被帶到警局去了。

發音重點 強調原因 police's requirements 以及結果 taken into the police station。requirement 的 qu 發音是 [kw]。

---

2 Because **I was tired**, I **didn't go**.

因為我很累，所以我沒有去。

發音重點 強調原因 I was tried 以及結果 didn't go。

---

3 Mary **got that job** because she was the **best interviewee**.

瑪莉得到了那份工作，因為她是最棒的接受面試者。

發音重點 強調結果 got that job 以及原因 best interviewee，其中
interviewee 的 ee 發 [i] 的音。

・・・・・・・・・・・・・・・・・・・・・・・・・・・・・・

④ Charles was **absent from work** <u>because of</u>
sickness.

查爾斯因為生病而缺席了。

發音重點 強調結果 absent from work 以及原因 sickness。

・・・・・・・・・・・・・・・・・・・・・・・・・・・・・・

⑤ Cancer may **result from smoking frequently**.

癌症可能因經常吸煙造成。

發音重點 強調造成結果的原因 result from smoking frequently，其中
frequently 的發音是 [`frikwəntlı]，要多練習這個常考字。

・・・・・・・・・・・・・・・・・・・・・・・・・・・・・・

⑥ The failure was **due to a <u>careless attitude</u>**.

這次失敗是由於疏忽的態度造成的。

發音重點 強調原因 due to a careless attitude。

・・・・・・・・・・・・・・・・・・・・・・・・・・・・・・

⑦ The delay was **due to the bad weather**.

延誤是由於壞天氣造成的。

發音重點 強調原因 due to the bad weather。

・・・・・・・・・・・・・・・・・・・・・・・・・・・・・・

8 Linda contributes her success to **great efforts at work**.

琳達將她的成功歸因於她在工作上的努力。

發音重點 強調原因 great efforts at work。

9 Sam got stopped by the police **because he was drunk driving**.

山姆因為酒醉駕車而被警察攔了下來。

發音重點 強調原因 because he was drunk driving。

第 6 類

時間句 (Sentences with time phrases)

0-40.mp3　發音提示　粗體套色字為重音，加底線者為連音。

1　She **got married** <u>as soon as</u> she **left university**.

她一離開大學就結婚了。

發音重點　強調 got married 與 left university。

2　<u>Would you</u> still **keep your promise** when you know the **truth**?

當你知道實情時，你仍然會守住你的承諾嗎？

發音重點　特別強調主要子句中的 keep your promise。

③ **What** <u>would you</u> like to **have** when you <u>have a</u> **coffee break**?

在咖啡休息時間，你會想要吃或喝什麼？

發音重點 特別強調主要子句中的 have。

- -

④ You **shouldn't** <u>eat any</u> **more pie** before you have dinner.

你在吃晚餐前不應該再吃更多派了。

發音重點 強調不應該的事情 shouldn't eat any more pie。

- -

⑤ We'd better **catch up** with them before we do this.

我們在做這件事之前最好先趕上他們。

發音重點 強調主要子句的 catch up。

- -

⑥ **Her son should** have been **punished** after he did the wrong thing.

她的兒子在做錯事之後應該被懲罰的。

發音重點 強調主要子句 her son should have been punished。

- -

7 **Watch for <u>changes</u>** in weather before going out.

在外出前注意天氣的變化。

發音重點 強調主要子句 watch for changes in weather。

● ●

8 **Test** the **<u>strength</u>** of the **rope** before using it.

在使用繩子前要測試它的強度。

發音重點 強調主要子句 test the strength of the rope。

● ●

第 7 類

條件句與假設句 (Conditional sentences)

0-41.mp3　發音提示　粗體套色字為重音，加底線者為連音。

1　If the rain stops, **we'll be able to go for a walk**.

如果雨停，我們就可以去散步。

發音重點　強調結果 we'll be able to go for a walk。

2　If you study hard, **you'll surely pass the test**.

如果你用功讀書，你一定會通過考試。

發音重點　強調結果 you'll surely pass the test。

3　If you'd like to come over, **you're more than welcome**.

如果你想要來的話，很歡迎你來。

發音重點　強調結果 you're more than welcome。

4

Howard will certainly succeed **if he continues the way he is working now.**

如果霍華繼續像現在一樣努力的話，他一定會成功。

發音重點 強調條件 if he continues the way he is working now。

5

Should you fail, **don't feel discouraged.**

萬一你失敗了，不要覺得氣餒。

發音重點 強調結果 don't feel discouraged。

6

If I had your build, **I'd go out for the wrestling team.**

要是我有你的體格，我就會去參加摔角隊了。

發音重點 強調結果 I'd go out for the wrestling team。

7

If Diana had a ticket, **she would go to the movie with us.**

要是黛安娜有票的話，她就會和我們一起去看電影了。

發音重點 強調結果 she would go to the movie with us。

8   If my friend gave me ten dollars, **I <u>could afford</u> to <u>get a</u> bus ticket**.

要是我的朋友給我十元，我就買得起巴士的票了。

發音重點 強調結果 I could afford to get a bus ticket。

第 8 類

比較句 (Comparative sentences)

0-42.mp3 發音提示 粗體套色字為重音,加底線者為連音。

1 JR is **as famous as** JC.

JR 和 JC 一樣有名。

發音重點 強調一樣有名 as famous as。

2 A tiger is **as dangerous as** a lion.

老虎和獅子一樣危險。

發音重點 強調一樣危險 as dangerous as。

3 The book over there is **as interesting as** the one here.

那裡的書和這裡的一樣有趣。

發音重點 強調一樣有趣 as interesting as。

75

4 I understand him **as <u>well as</u>** you do.

我和你一樣了解他。

發音重點 強調一樣好 as well as。

．．．．．．．．．．．．．．．．．．．．．．．．．．．．．．

5 A bicycle is **<u>not as expensive as</u>** a car.

腳踏車沒有車子那麼貴。

發音重點 強調不一樣貴 not as expensive as。

．．．．．．．．．．．．．．．．．．．．．．．．．．．．．．

6 In this city, the sky is **not so blue <u>as</u>** it used to be.

在這個城市，天空不像以前那麼藍。

發音重點 強調不一樣藍 not so blue as。

．．．．．．．．．．．．．．．．．．．．．．．．．．．．．．

7 He has **<u>twice as</u> many <u>books as</u>** I have.

他有我兩倍的書。

發音重點 強調兩倍 twice as many books as。

．．．．．．．．．．．．．．．．．．．．．．．．．．．．．．

8 The box by the chair is **four times as** heavy as this suitcase.

椅子旁的箱子有這行李箱的四倍重。

發音重點 強調四倍 four times as heavy as。

9 Doctor Brown is **taller than** his students.

伯朗博士比他的學生高。

發音重點 強調比較高 taller than。

10 You've heard **as much news as** I have.

你聽過的消息和我一樣多。

發音重點 強調一樣多 as much news as。

11 We decided to drive **forty miles farther** before stopping.

我們決定在停止前再多開 40 英里的路。

發音重點 強調更遠 forty miles farther。

Chapter 2
考題透視

Part 1
朗讀短文

高分技巧

1. 先深呼吸，放鬆自己的心情。

2. 迅速瀏覽一遍所要閱讀的文章，抓出不會唸或較難發音的單字。

3. 根據文章內容改變朗誦語氣。

4. 遇到不太會唸的單字，請嘗試用字母拼音方式唸出。

5. 保持語調自然，注意掌握時間，不宜因時間限制犧牲發音準確性而加速朗讀，亦不宜因過度強調發音而無法於限制時間內唸完文章。

致勝關鍵 KeyPoints

　　第一部分朗讀題，通常會有兩段不同的文章，總字數大約 150 字左右。開始之前有 1 分鐘的準備時間，然後有 2 分鐘可以朗讀，但對於一般的母語人士而言，用平常說話的速度大約 80 秒就能唸完，時間可以說相當充裕，所以不需要刻意加快速度。唸得太快的話，反而可能發生中途思考發音而停頓的情況，甚至因為不小心口誤而重唸，給人不熟練的印象。最好的作法是在準備時間快速默唸一遍，開始錄音時則是配合自己眼睛閱讀和嘴巴發音的速度，不急不徐地朗讀，儘量避免因為太過急躁而發生失誤。（以下皆以單篇文章各 1 分鐘進行練習）

最常考主
題短文 *1*

Employee Training Program
員工訓練

主題短文

說明：請先利用 30 秒的時間閱讀下面的短文，然後在 1 分鐘內以正常的速度，
　　　清楚正確的讀出下面的短文，閱讀時請不要發出聲音。

　　A company wants its employees to take an English speaking training class. The management and staff must decide whether classes should be in normal working time or outside office hours. According to the result of the survey, almost 90% of employees want to take English lessons during the normal working time. Only 9% of employees want to take these classes outside office hours.

1-01.mp3 發音提示 粗體套色字為重音，加底線者為連音。

A **company** wants its **employees** to take an **English speaking training class**. The **management** and **staff** must **decide** whether **classes** should be in **normal working time** or **outside office hours**. **According** to the **result** of the **survey**, almost **ninety percent** of employees want to take **English lessons** during the **normal working time**. **Only nine percent** of **employees** want to **take** these classes **outside office hours**.

中文理解　　　　　一家公司想要它的員工上英語口說訓練課。管理階層和員工必須決定課程應該在正常工作時間還是在辦公時間以外。根據調查的結果，幾乎百分之九十的員工想要在正常工作時間上英語課。只有百分之九的員工想在辦公時間外上這些課。

學習解析

❶ employee [ˌɛmplɔɪ`i] 雇員 n.

❷ training [`trenɪŋ] 訓練 n.

❸ management [`mænɪdʒmənt] 管理階層 n.

❹ staff [stæf] 全體員工（總稱） n.

❺ normal working time 平常上班時間

❻ outside office hours 在上班時間外

❼ survey [`sɝve] 調查 n.

致勝關鍵 KeyPoints

★一天上班各種活動的說法：

活動	英文
打卡上班	punch in（美式）/ clock in（英式）
開會	have a meeting
中午休息	take a lunch break
打卡下班	punch out（美式）/ clock out（英式）
加班	work overtime

最常考主
題短文 *2*

Child Care Program at University

大學的孩童托育方案

主題短文

說明：請先利用 30 秒的時間閱讀下面的短文，然後在 1 分鐘內以正常的速度，
　　　清楚正確的讀出下面的短文，閱讀時請不要發出聲音。

At our university, we offer three different programs for students who have
children. We have a day care program for infants from 3 months to 20
months. We have another program for children between 2 to 5 years of age,
and we also have an after-school program for elementary school children. If
any of you, new students, need these services, please let me know at once so
we can get you an application form.

1-02.mp3 發音提示　粗體套色字為重音，加底線者為連音。

At **our** university, we **offer❶** three different **programs** for **students** who
have **children**. We have a **day care program❷** for **infants❸** from **three**

months to **twenty months**. We have another **program** for **children** between **two to five** years of age, and we also have an **after-school** program for ④ elementary school children. If **any** of you, new **students**, need these ⑤ services, please **let me know** ⑥ at once so we can get you an ⑦ application form.

中文理解

　　在我們的大學，我們為有孩子的學生提供三個不同的方案。我們對於三個月到二十個月的嬰兒有一個日間托育方案。我們有另一個方案提供給二到五歲之間的小孩，而且我們也有給國小孩童的課後輔導方案。如果各位新生有任何人需要這些服務，請立刻讓我知道，好讓我們能提供申請表。

學習解析

❶ offer [`ɔfɚ] 提供 v.

❷ day care 日間托育

❸ infant [`ɪnfənt] 嬰兒 n.

❹ elementary school 國小

❺ service [`sɝvɪs] 服務 n.

❻ at once 立即地（副詞片語）

ex: Hearing the scream, he ran back home at once.

聽到尖叫聲時，他立即跑回家。

❼ application form 申請表

最常考主
題短文 *3*

Television 電視

主題短文

說明：請先利用 30 秒的時間閱讀下面的短文，然後在 1 分鐘內以正常的速度，
清楚正確的讀出下面的短文，閱讀時請不要發出聲音。

Television has some advantages and disadvantages. It keeps us informed
about the latest news and also provides entertainment in the home. On the
other hand, television has been blamed for causing the violent behavior of
some young people and encouraging children to sit indoors instead of getting
enough outdoor exercise.

1-03.mp3 （發音提示） 粗體套色字為重音，加底線者為連音。

Television has some ❶**advantages** and ❷**disadvantages**. It keeps us
❸**informed** about the **latest** news and also ❹**provides** ❺**entertainment** in the
home. On the other hand, **television** has been ❻**blamed** for causing the
❼**violent behavior** of some **young** people and ❽**encouraging children** to
sit indoors instead of getting enough ❾**outdoor exercise**.

中文理解 　　電視有一些優點跟缺點。它讓我們知道最新的消息，也提供在家裡的娛樂。另一方面，電視也被指責為造成一些年輕人暴力行為的原因，以及鼓勵孩子坐在室內，而不是進行足夠的戶外運動。

學習解析

❶ advantage [əd`væntɪdʒ] 優點 n.

❷ disadvantage [͵dɪsəd`væntɪdʒ] 缺點 n.

❸ inform [ɪn`fɔrm] 告知 v.

❹ provide [prə`vaɪd] 提供 v.

❺ entertainment [͵ɛntə`tenmənt] 娛樂 n.

❻ blame [blem] 責怪 v.

❼ violent [`vaɪələnt] 暴力的 adj.

❽ encourage [ɪn`kɝɪdʒ] 鼓勵 v.

❾ outdoor exercise 戶外運動

致勝關鍵 KeyPoints

★常見數字模式的唸法：

數字顯示	數字唸法
12%	twelve percent
1/2	half
2/3	two thirds
3/4	three quarters
0.314	zero point three one four

最常考主
題短文 4

Sports 運動

主題短文

說明：請先利用 30 秒的時間閱讀下面的短文，然後在 1 分鐘內以正常的速度，
　　　清楚正確的讀出下面的短文，閱讀時請不要發出聲音。

　　Sports are good for both body and mind. A person who seldom exercises will not only get sick very easily but have slow reflexes as well. Frankly speaking, an ill person can't study efficiently. A "slow motion" person has a hard time handling sudden changes. Therefore, doing sports is necessary for everyone. Let's do it right now.

1-04.mp3 （發音提示） 粗體套色字為重音，加底線者為連音。

Sports are **good** for both ❶body and ❷mind. A person who ❸seldom **exercises** will not only get **sick** very **easily** but have slow ❹reflexes as well. ❺Frankly speaking, an **ill person** can't **study** ❻efficiently. A "slow ❼motion" person has a **hard time** handling **sudden changes**. **Therefore**, doing sports is **necessary** for **everyone**. **Let's** do it **right now**.

中文理解

　　運動對於身心都有幫助。一個很少做運動的人不僅非常容易生病，反應能力也會比較慢。坦白地說，生病的人不能有效率地學習。一個「慢動作」的人則會對處理突然的變化感到棘手。因此，做運動對於每個人來說都是必要的。讓我們現在就做運動吧。

學習解析

❶ body [`bɑdɪ] 身體 n.

❷ mind [maɪnd] 心智 n.

❸ seldom [`sɛldəm] 很少地 adv.

❹ reflexes [`riflɛksɪz] 反應能力 n.

❺ frankly [`fræŋklɪ] 坦白地 adv.

❻ efficiently [ɪ`fɪʃəntlɪ] 有效率地 adv.

❼ motion [`moʃən] 動作 n.

最常考主
題短文 *5*

Swimming 游泳

主題短文

說明：請先利用 30 秒的時間閱讀下面的短文，然後在 1 分鐘內以正常的速度，
　　　清楚正確的讀出下面的短文，閱讀時請不要發出聲音。

I enjoy playing baseball, basketball, tennis and table tennis. My favorite
sport, though, is swimming. When you swim, you actually exercise almost
every muscle of your body. There are two great things that swimming can do
for you. In summer, swimming can cool you down, and in winter it helps
you adjust to cold weather.

1-05.mp3 發音提示　粗體套色字為重音，加底線者為連音。

I **enjoy** playing **baseball**, **basketball**, **tennis** and **table tennis**. My
favorite sport, though, is **swimming**. When you **swim**, you ❶**actually**
exercise almost **every** ❷**muscle** of your body. There are **two great things**
that **swimming can do** for you. In **summer**, swimming can **cool** you
down, and in winter it helps you ❸**adjust** to **cold weather**.

 中文理解

我喜愛打棒球、籃球、網球和桌球。不過，我最喜歡的運動是游泳。當你游泳的時候，你實際上會動用到你身體幾乎每一條肌肉。游泳可以為你做到兩件很棒的事。在夏季，游泳能讓你覺得涼快，而在冬季，它能幫助你適應寒冷的天氣。

學習解析

❶ actually [`æktʃʊəlɪ] 實際上 adv.

❷ muscle [`mʌsl] 肌肉 n.

❸ adjust [ə`dʒʌst] 調整以適應 v.

致勝關鍵 KeyPoints

★常見「所以」的說法：

置於句首	置於句中
Therefore...	...and therefore...
Thus...	...and thus...
	...so...

最常考主
題短文 6

A Special Exhibition
特別的展覽

主題短文

說明：請先利用 30 秒的時間閱讀下面的短文，然後在 1 分鐘內以正常的速度，
清楚正確的讀出下面的短文，閱讀時請不要發出聲音。

　　The Chicago Museum of Science and Industry will be opening a special exhibition entitled "Aliens are coming soon." This exhibit focuses on how different our environment would be if aliens were coming to the Earth. It will start on Tue., Apr. 14, and will be open every day through June 12, from 9:00 to 5:30, except Mondays.

1-06.mp3 發音提示　粗體套色字為重音，加底線者為連音。

❶The Chicago Museum of Science and Industry will be opening a special ❷exhibition entitled "❸Aliens are coming soon." This exhibit focuses on how different our environment would be if aliens were coming to the Earth. It will start on Tuesday, April fourteenth, and will be open every day through June twelfth, from nine o'clock to five thirty, except Mondays.

中文理解　　　芝加哥科學及工業博物館將舉辦一場名為「外星人即將到來」的特別展覽會。這場展覽聚焦在如果外星人來到地球，我們的環境將會是多麼不同。它將在四月十四日星期二開始，並且到六月十二日為止每天九點到五點半開放，除了星期一以外。

學習解析

❶ the Chicago Museum of Science and Industry 芝加哥科學及工業博物館
❷ exhibition [ˌɛksə`bɪʃən] 展覽 n.
❸ alien [`elɪən] 外星人 n.

致勝關鍵 KeyPoints

★常見日期的唸法：

日期顯示	唸法	中譯
Jan. 1	January first	一月一日
Feb. 2	February second	二月二日
Mar. 3	March third	三月三日
Apr. 4	April fourth	四月四日
May 10	May tenth	五月十日
June 11	June eleventh	六月十一日
July 12	July twelfth	七月十二日
Aug. 13	August thirteenth	八月十三日
Sept. 20	September twentieth	九月二十日
Oct. 21	October twenty-first	十月二十一日
Nov. 22	November twenty-second	十一月二十二日

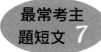

最常考主
題短文 7

A Narration 一段陳述

主題短文

說明：請先利用 30 秒的時間閱讀下面的短文，然後在 1 分鐘內以正常的速度，
清楚正確的讀出下面的短文，閱讀時請不要發出聲音。

I live in Boston now and visit my parents in Florida twice a year. Whenever I visit them, I spend many hours with them. I like to go to the beach nearby not only to swim in the sea, but also to relax and think. The waves are gentle, the water soothing. What is more important to me is the sea's peacefulness. I want to be calm like that.

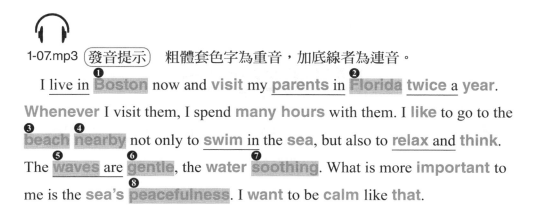

1-07.mp3 (發音提示) 粗體套色字為重音，加底線者為連音。

I live in **Boston** now and **visit** my **parents** in **Florida** twice a **year**. **Whenever** I visit them, I spend **many hours** with them. I **like** to go to the **beach nearby** not only to **swim** in the **sea**, but also to **relax** and **think**. The **waves** are **gentle**, the **water soothing**. What is more **important** to me is the **sea's peacefulness**. I **want** to be **calm** like **that**.

中文理解

　　我現在居住在波士頓，而且每年兩次到佛羅里達拜訪我爸媽。每當我拜訪時，我都花很多時間跟他們在一起。我喜歡去附近的海灘，不止為了在海裡游泳，也是為了放鬆和思考。海浪是柔和的，海水令人沉靜。但對我來說更重要的是大海的寧靜。我想要像海一樣平靜。

學習解析

❶ Boston [`bɔstn̩] 波士頓 n.

❷ Florida [`flɔrədə] 佛羅里達 n.

❸ beach [bitʃ] 海灘 n.

❹ nearby [`nɪrˏbaɪ] 附近的 adj.

❺ wave [wev] 海浪 n.

❻ gentle [`dʒɛntl̩] 柔和的 adj.

❼ soothing [`suðɪŋ] 令人沉靜的 adj.

❽ peacefulness [`pisfʊlnɪs] 寧靜 n.

致勝關鍵 KeyPoints

★常見年的唸法：

年的顯示	年的唸法
1900	nineteen hundred
1905	nineteen O five
2001	two thousand and one
2012	twenty twelve
1990's	nineteen nineties

最常考主
題短文 **8**

Wedding Reception

結婚宴會

主題短文

說明：請先利用 30 秒的時間閱讀下面的短文，然後在 1 分鐘內以正常的速度，
　　　清楚正確的讀出下面的短文，閱讀時請不要發出聲音。

A wedding reception is a big event. This is a big party after the ceremony. Everyone brings or sends a gift, so the young couple often doesn't need to buy a lot of things for their house. The wedding reception may be a dinner, or it may be a teatime party with only snacks. Champagne is usually served, and everyone eats, drinks, and dances for many hours. Anyway, everybody is happy at that time.

1-08.mp3 （發音提示）　粗體套色字為重音，加底線者為連音。

A ❶**wedding reception** is a ❷**big event**. This is a **big party** after the ❸**ceremony**. Everyone **brings** or **sends a** ❹**gift**, so the **young couple often** doesn't **need** to **buy** a lot of **things** for their **house**. The **wedding reception** may be a **dinner**, or it may be a ❺**teatime party** with only

⑥
snacks. **⑦**
Champagne is usually **⑧**
served, and **everyone eats**, **drinks**,
and **dances** for **many hours**. Anyway, **everybody** is **happy** at **that time**.

中文理解　　　　　　　結婚宴會是盛大的活動。這是（結婚）典禮之後的
大型派對。每個人會攜帶或者寄送一件禮物，所以年輕
夫婦通常不需要為房子買很多東西。結婚宴會可能是一頓晚餐，或者可能是只有
一些點心的茶會。會中通常會供應香檳酒，每個人會吃、喝及跳舞很多個小時。
不管怎樣，每個人在那個時候都很快樂。

學習解析

❶ wedding reception 結婚宴會
❷ event [ɪ`vɛnt] 活動 n.
❸ ceremony [`sɛrəˌmonɪ] 典禮 n.
❹ gift [gɪft] 禮物 n.
❺ teatime party 茶會
❻ snack [snæk] 點心 n.
❼ champagne [ʃæm`pen] 香檳 n.
❽ serve [sɝv] 供應食物 v.

最常考主
題短文 9

Salmon　鮭魚

主題短文

說明：請先利用 30 秒的時間閱讀下面的短文，然後在 1 分鐘內以正常的速度，
　　　清楚正確的讀出下面的短文，閱讀時請不要發出聲音。

　Salmon are fish which live a part of their lives in rivers and the other in
the sea. They lay their eggs in the gravel bottoms of streams. The young
salmon begin life in the streams and descend into the rivers. Finally, they
swim out to sea, where they feed and grow to full size. Then they swim
upstream to the same streams they were born in. There they lay their eggs.

1-09.mp3 (發音提示) 粗體套色字為重音，加底線者為連音。

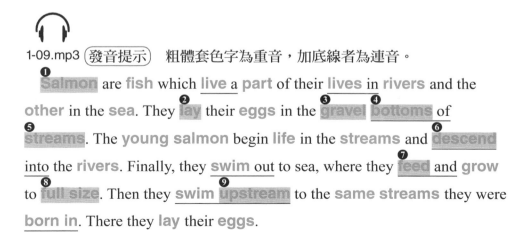

❶Salmon are **fish** which **live** a **part** of their **lives** in **rivers** and the
other in the **sea**. They **❷lay** their **eggs** in the **❸gravel ❹bottoms** of
❺streams. The **young salmon** begin **life** in the **streams** and **❻descend**
into the **rivers**. Finally, they **swim** out to sea, where they **❼feed** and **grow**
to **❽full size**. Then they **swim ❾upstream** to the **same streams** they were
born in. There they **lay** their **eggs**.

中文理解　　　　鮭魚是一種魚，牠們生命的一部分活在河中，另一部分在海中。牠們把卵產在溪流的礫石底部。年幼的鮭魚在溪流誕生，然後往下進入河川。最後，牠們游向海洋，在那裡覓食並且成長到成魚的大小。然後牠們往上游，到牠們出生的相同溪流。牠們在那裡產卵。

學習解析

❶ salmon [`sæmən] 鮭魚 n.

❷ lay [le] 產（卵）v.

❸ gravel [`grævl] 礫石 n.

❹ bottom [`bɑtəm] 底部 n.

❺ stream [strim] 溪流 n.

❻ descend [dɪ`sɛnd] 下降 v.

❼ feed [fid] 覓食 v.

❽ full size 成年的尺寸

❾ upstream [‚ʌp`strim] 往上游處 adv.

最常考主題
短文 *10*

Mother Teresa　泰瑞莎修女

主題短文

說明：請先利用 30 秒的時間閱讀下面的短文，然後在 1 分鐘內以正常的速度，
　　　清楚正確的讀出下面的短文，閱讀時請不要發出聲音。

Mother Teresa first worked as a schoolteacher in India, but her students were not poor people. In the end, she left the school. It was the start of her real life's work. She walked the streets in Indian cities in order to look for poor people. She gave them food, clothing or medicine. She was very nice to them.

1-10.mp3　發音提示　粗體套色字為重音，加底線者為連音。

Mother Teresa first worked <u>as a</u> **schoolteacher** in ❶**India**, but her **students** were not ❷**poor** people. In the **end**, she left the **school**. It was the start of her ❸**real life's work**. She ❹**walked** the **streets** in **Indian** cities in ❺**order** to ❻**look** for poor people. She **gave** them **food**, ❻**clothing** or ❼**medicine**. She was very **nice** to them.

中文理解

　　一開始泰瑞莎修女在印度擔任學校教師的工作，但她的學生並不是貧窮的人。最後，她離開了學校。這就是她開始真正的畢生工作的時候。為了尋找貧苦的人，她在印度城市街上遊走。她給他們食物、衣物或者藥品。她對他們非常好。

學習解析

❶ India [`ɪndɪə] 印度 n.

❷ poor [pʊr] 窮困的 adj.

❸ real [`riəl] 真正的 adj.

❹ walk the streets 在街上遊走（動詞片語）

ex: After having dinner, I walked the streets in New York.

吃完晚餐後，我在紐約的街上遊走。

（註："walk the streets" 有另一個舊意和隱意為當妓女，國內很多字典都有收錄這個意思，然而現今的用法大多是「在街上遊走」。若強解為「當妓女」，則有許多句子的翻譯不但會與原意不合，還會貽笑大方。）

❺ look for 尋找（動詞片語）

ex: What are you looking for? 你在找什麼？

❻ clothing [`kloðɪŋ] 衣服（總稱） n.

❼ medicine [`mɛdəsn̩] 藥品 n.

最常考主題
短文 *11*

Medical Costs in the USA
美國的醫療費用

主題短文

說明：請先利用 30 秒的時間閱讀下面的短文，然後在 1 分鐘內以正常的速度，
清楚正確的讀出下面的短文，閱讀時請不要發出聲音。

　　Medical costs in the USA are very high. The cost of a hospital stay can be
as much as $200 per day or even more. The costs of medicines and medical
tests are also high. The family of the patient is responsible for these
expenses. Consequently, it would be a terrible financial burden for them for
a long time.

1-11.mp3　發音提示　粗體套色字為重音，加底線者為連音。

　　Medical ❶costs in the **USA** are **very high**. The cost of a **hospital
stay** can be as **much** as **two hundred dollars** per **day** or **even** more.
The **costs** of **medicines** and ❷**medical tests** are also **high**. The family of
❸the **patient** is **responsible** for these ❹**expenses**. ❺**Consequently**, it
would be a **terrible financial burden** for them for a **long time**.

PART 1

中文理解 ⋯⋯⋯⋯ 美國的醫療費用很高。住院的費用可能會多達每天兩百美元甚至更多。藥和醫學檢測的費用也很高。病患的家屬要負責這些花費。因此，這會長期成為他們可怕的財務負擔。

學習解析

❶ cost [kɔst] 花費 n.
❷ medical test 醫學檢測
❸ patient [`peʃənt] 病人 n.
❹ expense [ɪk`spɛns] 費用 n.
❺ consequently [`kɑnsəˌkwɛntlɪ] 結果是 adv.

致勝關鍵 KeyPoints

★常見各國幣值的唸法：

幣值	唸法
$625	six hundred and twenty-five dollars
$1.25	one dollar and twenty-five cents (one twenty-five)
US$25	twenty-five US dollars
NT$100	one hundred NT dollars
¥1,250	one thousand two hundred and fifty Japanese yen
€ 51	fifty-one euros
£2.67	two pounds and sixty-seven pence

Chapter 2
考題透視

Part 2
回答問題

高分技巧

1. 先深呼吸，放鬆自己的心情。

2. 注意聆聽問題，尤其第一個字一定要注意聽，
   免得發生題目問「哪裡」你卻回答「什麼時候」
   之類的情況。

3. 答題切勿慌張，咬字要清楚，避免因咬字不清，
   而讓評分老師無法理解或聽成別的東西。

4. 當結束鈴聲響起，請立刻停止回答，不要為了
   把答案說完而漏聽了下一題。

PART 2

Your Favorites 1 你的最愛（一）

主題說明

這是一個已經被考到爛掉的主題，但也是你不得不會的一種題目，通常這種考題會用 what 或 who 的問題來問你喜歡的東西或人物，並且要求你說明原因或加以描述。

常見問句句型

1. What is your favorite ~?

   你最喜歡的⋯是什麼？

2. Who is your favorite ~?

   你最喜歡的⋯是誰？

3. Where is your favorite ~?

   你最喜歡的⋯是哪裡？

4. Can you describe your favorite ~?

   你能夠描述一下你最喜歡的⋯嗎？

5. Do you have a favorite ~?

   你有最喜歡的⋯嗎？

常見回答句型

1. My favorite ~ is ~ because ~

我最喜歡的…是…，因為…

2. I like ~ most ~ because ~

我最喜歡…，因為…

3. Well, in fact, I don't have a favorite ~. I think ~.

嗯，事實上，我沒有最喜歡的…我認為…

4. Definitely! ~ is my favorite ~. I am crazy for ~.

當然！…是我最愛的…。我為…而瘋狂。

5. Many people like ~, but my favorite ~ is ~

很多人喜歡…，但我最愛的…是…

考 題 測 試 >>>>

答題示範 🎧 2-01.mp3　模擬測驗 🎧 2-01-Q.mp3

這個部份共有十題。題目已事先錄音，每題經由耳機播出二次，不印在試卷上。第一至五題，每題回答時間 15 秒；第六至十題，每題回答時間 30 秒。每題播出後，請立即回答。回答時，不一定要用完整句子，但請在作答時間內盡量的表達。（可先聽答題示範音檔，再用模擬測驗音檔進行練習）

1 What is your favorite type of TV program? Why do you like it?

你最喜歡的電視節目是什麼？為什麼你喜歡它？

My favorite type of TV program❶ is the news report because it lets me know what is happening around the globe❷, which makes me feel like I'm connected❸ to the world.

我最喜歡的電視節目是新聞報導，因為它讓我知道全世界發生的事，這讓我覺得我和世界有所連結。

105

學習解析

❶ TV program 電視節目

❷ around the globe 在全世界

❸ be connected to 和…相連

致勝關鍵 KeyPoints

★電視節目的類型：

英文	中文	知名頻道或節目
news	新聞	CNN、BBC、TVBS、Next TV（壹電視）、EBC News（東森新聞）、SET News（三立新聞）
cartoon	卡通	Cartoon Network、Animax、Disney Channel
sports	運動	VL Sports（緯來體育台）、ELTA TV（愛爾達電視）、Eleven Sports
documentary	記錄紀實	Discovery、Animal Planet、National Geographic
music	音樂	MTV、Channel V
series	連續劇	Sex and the City（慾望城市）、Game of Thrones（權力遊戲）、Someday or One Day（想見你）

2 What is your favorite Website? What do you often do on it?

你最喜歡的網站是什麼？你常常在上面做什麼？

 My favorite **Website**❶ is Google. I often **search**❷ for information I'm interested in on it, and it also provides free email service with a large **storage capacity**❸.

我最喜歡的網站是 Google。我常常在上面搜尋我有興趣的資訊，它也提供有很大儲存空間的免費電子郵件服務。

學習解析

❶ Website [`wɛb͵saɪt] 網站 n.

❷ search [sɝtʃ] 搜尋 v.

❸ storage capacity 儲存容量

3 What is your favorite animal? Why do you like it?

你最喜歡的動物是什麼？為什麼你喜歡牠？

 My favorite animal is the dog. I like dogs because they are **loyal**❶ and can do a lot of things for **human beings**❷.

我最喜歡的動物是狗。我喜歡狗是因為牠們很忠心，而且可以幫人類做很多事情。

Many people like cats and dogs, but my favorite animal is the tiger. I think tigers are strong and **powerful**❸, and they look very beautiful.

許多人喜歡貓跟狗，但是我最喜歡的動物是老虎。我認為老虎既強壯又有力，而且牠們看起來非常美。

PART 2

學習解析

❶ loyal [`lɔɪəl] 忠心的 adj.

❷ human beings 人類

❸ powerful [`pɑʊə-fəl] 強而有力的 adj.

致勝關鍵 KeyPoints

★其他動物的說法：

英文	中文	常見的相關形容詞
sheep	綿羊	peaceful（和平的）、tame（溫馴的）
lion	獅子	strong（強壯的）、cruel（殘忍的）
rabbit	兔子	cute（可愛的）、sensitive（敏感的）、sneaky（狡猾的）
cat	貓	independent（獨立的）、clean（乾淨的）、quiet（安靜的）
bird	鳥	free（自由的）、colorful（色彩繽紛的）

4 What is your favorite country? What is special about the country?

你最喜愛的國家是什麼？這個國家有什麼特別的地方？

I like the United Kingdom the most. It's a country with a long history. It is also the place where the industrial revolution began, so it has been the most influential country in the world.

我最喜歡英國。它是歷史悠久的國家。它也是工業革命開始的地方，所以它曾經是世界上最有影響力的國家。

108

學習解析

❶ the United Kingdom 聯合王國（英國的正式稱呼）

❷ industrial revolution 工業革命

❸ influential [ˌɪnflʊ`ɛnʃəl] 有影響力的 adj.

 What is your favorite drink in the summer? Why do you like it?

你在夏天最喜歡的飲料是什麼？為什麼你喜歡它？

 I like ❶watermelon juice. I think it's sweet and natural. After staying outside in hot weather for hours, a glass of cold watermelon juice really makes you feel ❷refreshed.

我喜歡西瓜汁。我覺得它又甜又自然。在炎熱的天氣長時間待在外面之後，一杯冰涼的西瓜汁真的會讓你覺得恢復了活力。

學習解析

❶ watermelon [`wɔtɚˌmɛlən] 西瓜 n.

❷ refreshed [rɪ`frɛʃt] 恢復了活力的 adj.

致勝關鍵 KeyPoints

★其他飲料的說法：

英文	中文	英文	中文
coke	可樂	papaya milkshake / papaya milk smoothie	木瓜牛奶
beer	啤酒	grass jelly drink	仙草蜜
mineral water	礦泉水	aiyu jelly drink	愛玉冰
soda	汽水	bubble tea	珍珠奶茶
lemonade	檸檬水	winter melon tea	冬瓜茶

6 What is your favorite style of food? Why do you like it? Tell me about it.

你最喜歡的是哪種料理？你為什麼喜歡它？告訴我關於它的事。

Chinese food is my favorite because it's full of **variety**. For example, a piece of **tofu** can be made into **fried** tofu, vegetable soup with tofu, cold tofu dressed with **soy sauce** and many other kinds of dishes. Also, many foreigners are amazed by the various cooking **techniques** that Chinese use. That's why Chinese food keeps **evolving** and gaining **popularity** around the world.

中式料理是我的最愛，因為它充滿了變化。例如，一塊豆腐可以被做成炸豆腐、青菜豆腐湯、醬油涼拌豆腐和其他許多種菜色。還有，許多外國人對於華人使用的各種烹飪技巧而感到驚奇。這就是中式料理之所以持續演進，並且在全世界越來越受歡迎的原因。

學習解析

❶ variety [vəˋraɪətɪ] 多樣性 n.

❷ tofu [ˋtofu] 豆腐 n.

❸ fry [fraɪ] 炸 v.

❹ soy sauce 醬油

❺ technique [tɛkˋnik] 技術 n.

❻ evolve [ɪˋvɑlv] 進化 v.

❼ popularity [ˌpɑpjəˋlærətɪ] 流行，受歡迎 n.

7 What is your favorite holiday? Why do you like it?

你最喜歡的節日是什麼？為什麼你喜歡它？

 It depends on where I am. If I were American, my favorite holiday would be Christmas because I can get lots of gifts on that day. However, since I am Taiwanese, I love Chinese New Year more. It's the time of the year when I can get lucky money from my relatives.

取決於我在哪裡。如果我是美國人，我最愛的節日會是聖誕節，因為我在那一天可以得到很多禮物。不過，因為我是台灣人，所以我比較喜歡華人的新年。這是一年之中我可以從親戚那邊得到壓歲錢的時候。

學習解析

❶ depend on 取決於…

❷ gift [gɪft] 禮物

❸ lucky money 壓歲錢

PART 2

致勝關鍵 KeyPoints

★其他節日的說法：

英文	中文
New Year's Eve	跨年夜
Chinese New Year / Lunar New Year	華人新年／陰曆新年
Lantern Festival	元宵節
Tomb-Sweeping Day	清明節
Mother's Day	母親節
Dragon Boat Festival	端午節
Qixi Festival	七夕
Ghost Festival	中元節
Mid-Autumn Festival	中秋節
Easter	復活節
All Saints Day	萬聖節
Halloween	萬聖節前夜
Thanksgiving	感恩節
Christmas	聖誕節

8 What is your favorite kind of book? Can you talk about it?

你最喜歡哪種書？可以談談有關於它的事情嗎？

 I like novels, and I like reading them in bed. However, the habit
 affects my sleep quality sometimes, especially when the story is very

❹exciting. Once I read "Harry Potter" all night, and I just couldn't put it down. When I lifted my head from the book, it was 8 o'clock in the morning already.

我喜歡小說，而且喜歡在床上讀。然而，這個習慣有時候會影響我的睡眠品質，尤其當故事非常刺激的時候。有一次我讀了整晚的《哈利波特》，我就是不能把它放下。當我把我的頭從書中抬起來，已經是早上八點鐘了。

學習解析

❶ novel [`nɑvḷ] 小說 n.

❷ affect [ə`fɛkt] 影響 v.

❸ sleep quality 睡眠品質

❹ exciting [ɪk`saɪtɪŋ] 刺激的 adj.

致勝關鍵 KeyPoints

★其他書籍種類的說法：

英文	中文
English/Japanese study book	英文／日文學習書
comic book	漫畫書
guidebook	旅遊導覽書
encyclopedia	百科全書
novel/fiction	小說
science fiction (SF)	科幻小說
fantasy	奇幻小說（中古騎士與魔法之類的小說）
wuxia fiction	武俠小說

romance	愛情小說
investing book	投資書
self-help book	心理勵志書

9 What is your favorite kind of movie? Why do you like it?

你最喜歡哪種電影？你為什麼喜歡它？

Although my boyfriend hates thrillers❶, I really love them. My job is kind of boring❷, so I think that's why I like to find something scary❸ when I go to the movies. Also, when I see a thriller with my boyfriend, he always looks more frightened❹ than me, which makes me feel superior❺.

雖然我的男朋友討厭驚悚片，但是我真的很愛。我的工作有點無聊，所以我想那就是我去電影院看電影時喜歡找恐怖的片子的原因。還有，當我和男朋友看驚悚片時，他看起來總是比我害怕，這讓我覺得比他優越。

學習解析

❶ thriller [ˋθrɪlɚ] 驚悚片，驚悚小說 n.

❷ boring [ˋborɪŋ] 令人無聊的 adj.

❸ scary [ˋskɛrɪ] 可怕的，嚇人的 adj.

❹ frightened [ˋfraɪtn̩d] 受到驚嚇的，覺得害怕的 adj.

❺ superior [səˋpɪrɪɚ] 比較優越的 adj.

致勝關鍵 KeyPoints

★其他電影種類的說法：

英文	中文
thriller	驚悚片
horror movie	恐怖片
war movie	戰爭片
comedy	喜劇片
action movie	動作片
animation	動畫片／卡通片
romance movie	愛情片

10 What is your favorite kind of music? What do you like about it?

你最愛的音樂種類是什麼？你喜歡它的什麼方面？

I like ❶pop music very much. Even though some people ❷criticize that the ❸lyrics of pop songs are always about love and the ❹melodies sound the same, it's ❺undeniable that they are easy to listen and dance to.

When I sing a pop song and move to the rhythm, I feel less ❻stressed. 我非常喜歡流行音樂。儘管有些人批評流行歌曲的歌詞總是關於愛情，而且旋律聽起來都一樣，但不能否認它們很容易聆聽以及跟著跳舞。當我唱流行歌曲並且跟著節奏擺動時，我覺得比較沒有壓力。

學習解析

❶ pop music 流行音樂

❷ criticize [`krɪtɪˌsaɪz] 批評 v.

❸ lyrics [`lɪrɪks] 歌詞 n.

❹ melody [`mɛlədɪ] 旋律 n.

❺ undeniable [ˌʌndɪ`naɪəbl̩] 無可否認的 adj.

❻ stressed [strɛst] 感到有壓力的 adj.

致勝關鍵 KeyPoints

★其他音樂種類的說法：

英文	中文
rock music	搖滾樂
classical music	古典音樂
jazz music	爵士樂
rap music	饒舌音樂
country music	鄉村音樂
folk music	民俗音樂

最常考生
活主題 *2*

Your Favorites 2 你的最愛（二）

主題說明

之前已經跟各位讀者說明了，這是一個考試最常見的主題，也應該是最好發揮的，但並不是所有這類的題目都會用 "favorite" 來表達，在這個單元將會介紹一些其他詢問喜好的方式。另外，如果題目問的並不是你喜歡的事物，例如問「你最喜歡的電台」，但你平常不聽廣播，這時候與其硬著頭皮介紹自己根本不知道的東西，還不如直接說「我不聽廣播」，並且說明自己不聽的理由，這樣也是很好的回答。只要你說得出理由，就不必非得想出「最喜歡的」不可。

常見問句句型

1. Which ~ do you like best?
   你最喜歡哪個…？

2. Which ~ do you admire most?
   你最欣賞哪個…？

3. What ~ do you like most?
   你最喜歡什麼…？

4. What kind of ~ do you prefer?
   你比較喜歡哪種…？

5. What ~ do you love?
   你喜愛什麼…？

PART 2

常見回答句型

1. ~ is really my cup of tea!
   …真的很合我的胃口！

2. I am a fan of ~.
   我很迷…。

3. I love ~ very much.
   我非常喜愛…。

4. Among ~, I prefer ~.
   在…之中，我比較喜歡…。

5. Hmm, I have no idea about ~, but ~.
   嗯，關於…我沒有任何想法，不過…。

考題測試 >>>>

答題示範 2-02.mp3　模擬測驗 2-02-Q.mp3

這個部份共有十題。題目已事先錄音，每題經由耳機播出二次，不印在試卷上。第一至五題，每題回答時間 15 秒；第六至十題，每題回答時間 30 秒。每題播出後，請立即回答。回答時，不一定要用完整句子，但請在作答時間內盡量的表達。（可先聽答題示範音檔，再用模擬測驗音檔進行練習）

1 Which pop singer do you like best? Why do you like him or her?

你最喜歡哪位流行歌手？為什麼你喜歡他／她？

 I like A-mei because she always sings very powerfully, and she's always so nice to her fans. Recently she also took part in a lot of charitable activities, which makes me even crazier for her.
我喜歡阿妹，因為她總是唱得很有力量，而且她總是對歌迷很好。最近她也參加了很多慈善活動，讓我更加為她瘋狂。

學習解析

❶ powerfully [ˋpaʊɚfəlɪ] 有力量地 adv.

❷ fan [fæn] 迷，粉絲

❸ take part in 參加

❹ charitable activities 慈善活動

致勝關鍵 KeyPoints

　　本題問最喜歡的流行歌手，回答時以熟悉的人為主，不分國內外男女歌手，最好能夠再加上這位流行歌手最近的消息。如果真的沒有人選，也可以直接回答沒有，並且接著談自己對流行歌手沒有興趣的原因。

2 What kind of magazine do you like most? What do you like about it?

你最喜歡哪種雜誌？你喜歡它的什麼地方？

I like ❶fashion magazines. I can read about the latest ❷trends in fashion magazines, and there are always some ❸unique looks I've never thought about.

我喜歡時尚雜誌。我可以在時尚雜誌裡讀到最近的趨勢，而且裡面總是有一些我從來沒想過的獨特（穿搭）風貌。

學習解析

❶ fashion magazine 時尚雜誌

❷ trend [trɛnd] 趨勢 n.

❸ unique [ju`nik] 獨特的 adj.

致勝關鍵 KeyPoints

　　本題問最喜歡的雜誌,雜誌種類多,但在回答時最好選擇你能回答為什麼的答案。例如最喜歡旅遊雜誌(travel magazines),可以說因為它們介紹許多有趣的地方(introduce many interesting places);最喜歡八卦雜誌(gossip magazines),因為它們揭露名人的私生活(reveal celebrities' private life)。

3　What is your best childhood memory? Tell me about your experience.

你最好的兒時記憶是什麼?告訴我你的經驗。

 I can't remember my childhood❶ clearly, but I'm sure there was a little garden behind my old house. I used to❷ play with my friends there.
我對於童年時期的記憶不清楚,但我確定我舊家後面有一個小花園。我過去常在那裡和朋友玩。

學習解析

❶ childhood [`tʃaɪld͵hʊd] 童年時期 n.

❷ used to 過去經常

致勝關鍵 KeyPoints

★ "be used to" 與 "used to" 的比較：

1. "be used to" 是「習慣於 ...」的意思，"used to" 是「過去經常 ...」的意思：

    ex: I am used to rap music. 我習慣饒舌音樂了。

    I used to go to KTV every weekend. 我過去通常每個週末去 KTV。

2. "be used to" 後接名詞或動名詞，"used to" 後接原形動詞：

    ex: I am used to living in Canada. 我習慣住在加拿大了。

    I used to play chess. 我過去會玩西洋棋。

3. 建構疑問句時，"be used to" 的 be 動詞往前移，"used to" 在句首使用助動詞 "did" 並將 "used" 改為原形動詞 "use"。

    ex: Are you used to Sashimi? 你們習慣生魚片嗎？

    Did you use to work in IBM? 你過去在 IBM 工作嗎？

4 ## What radio station do you like most? Why do you like it?

你最喜歡的電台是什麼？為什麼你喜歡它？

I like ICRT. The DJs there talk smoothly❶, and the stories they tell are interesting. More importantly, I can improve❷ my English by learning from them.

我喜歡 ICRT。那裡的 DJ 說話很流暢，他們說的故事也很有趣。更重要的是，我可以藉由向他們學習來增進自己的英語能力。

學習解析

❶ smoothly [smuðlɪ] 流暢地 adv.

❷ improve [ɪm`pruv] 改善，增進 v.

致勝關鍵 KeyPoints

★喜歡某一電台的原因有：

獲得最新的新聞資訊	get the latest news
聽好聽的流行音樂	listen to some good popular music
聽股市訊息	listen to some information about stock markets

5 What season do you love? What do you like to do at that time?

你喜愛什麼季節？你喜歡在那時候做什麼？

I like summer. In summer, I like to swim and eat ice cream. Also, the ❶ summer vacation is very long, so I can take a ❷ long-term trip.

我喜歡夏天。在夏天，我喜歡游泳和吃冰淇淋。還有，暑假非常長，所以我可以進行長時間的旅行。

學習解析

❶ summer vacation 暑假

❷ long-term [`lɔŋˌtɝm] 長期的 adj.

致勝關鍵 KeyPoints

★喜歡其他季節可能的原因：

最喜歡春季	spring
許多花朵綻放	many flowers are in bloom
最喜歡冬季	winter
吃火鍋	eat hot pots
最喜歡秋季	fall/autumn
不會太熱也不會太冷	it's not too hot or too cold

6 What sport do you like to play? Tell me about your experience.

你喜歡做什麼運動？告訴我你的經驗。

I like playing tennis❶. Tennis is my thing. When I have free time, I usually invite some good friends to play tennis with me. I play better than them, so sometimes I become their coach❷. If I have a chance, I will definitely attend❸ a tennis match❹.

我喜歡打網球。網球是我喜歡做的事。當我有空閒時間的時候，我通常會邀請一些好朋友和我打網球。我打得比他們好，所以有時候我會成為他們的教練。如果我有機會的話，我一定會到場看網球比賽。

學習解析

❶ tennis [ˋtɛnɪs] 網球 n.

PART 2

❷ coach [kotʃ] 教練 n.

❸ attend [əˋtɛnd] 出席（在這裡指到場觀看比賽） v.

❹ match [mætʃ] （雙方的）比賽 n.

致勝關鍵 KeyPoints

★各種活動的說法：

play	do	go	其他動詞
play basketball 打籃球	do exercise 做運動	go jogging 去慢跑	work out in a gym 在健身房健身
play volleyball 打排球	do yoga 做瑜伽	go swimming 去游泳	run on a treadmill 在跑步機上跑
play baseball 打棒球	do Tai Chi 打太極拳	go hiking 去健行	
play pool 打撞球	do aerobics 跳有氧舞蹈	go camping 去露營	

7 What is your favorite time of day? Why do you like it? What do you do at that time?

你最喜歡一天之中的什麼時候？為什麼喜歡？你在那個時候會做什麼？

Morning is the best time of day. I think I'm really a morning person. People say that the early bird catches the worm, so I treasure every hour in the morning. As soon as I get up, I start to do some exercise, and then I read some books in English to improve my English ability.

124

早上是一天之中最好的時光。我想我真的是一個晨型人。人們說早起的鳥兒有蟲吃，所以我珍惜早上的每一個小時。我一起床就開始做些運動，然後我會讀一些英文書來增進我的英文能力。

學習解析

❶ the early bird catches the worm 早起的鳥兒有蟲吃
❷ treasure [`trɛʒɚ] 珍惜 v.
❸ improve [ɪm`pruv] 改善，增進 v.

致勝關鍵 KeyPoints

★其他時段喜歡的原因舉例：

最喜歡晚上	evening
我可以在家休息	I can relax at home
最喜歡下午	afternoon
我可以和朋友一起喝下午茶	I can have a tea break with my friends

8 Which actor do you like most? Why do you like him?

你最喜歡哪位男演員？你為什麼喜歡他？

Hmm, I'm not familiar with movie stars, but I kind of like Leonardo DiCaprio. He looks charming and nice. His smile must be attractive to many women. I'm not really a fan, but for me, his handsome face stands out among all the actors. Even though I only saw a few of his movies, there is no doubt he gave me a deep impression.❹

嗯，我對電影明星不熟悉，但我蠻喜歡李奧納多·迪卡皮歐的。他看起來很迷人，而且人很好的樣子。他的微笑對於許多女性而言一定很有吸引力。我不是真正的粉絲，但對我而言，他英俊的臉在所有演員當中很突出。儘管我只看過他的幾部電影，但毫無疑問地，他帶給我很深的印象。

學習解析

❶ charming [`tʃɑrmɪŋ] 迷人的 adj.
❷ attractive [ə`træktɪv] 有吸引力的 adj.
❸ stand out 突出
❹ impression [ɪm`prɛʃən] 印象 n.

9 Which actress do you like most? Why do you like her?

你最喜歡哪位女演員？你為什麼喜歡她？

I'm a fan of Scarlett Johansson. I have many posters❶ of her. She is absolutely❷ gorgeous❸, and her figure❹ is perfect. I also admire that she's not afraid to express❺ her political❻ views. And as everyone knows, she became very famous by playing "Black Widow" in Marvel movies, and I think her acting was impressive.❼

我是史嘉蕾·喬韓森的粉絲。我有她的許多海報。她真的超美的，而且她的身材很完美。我也欣賞她不怕表達自己的政治觀點。而就像每個人所知道的，她藉由扮演漫威電影中的「黑寡婦」而變得非常有名，我認為她的演出令人印象深刻。

學習解析

❶ poster [`postɚ] 海報 n.

❷ absolutely [`æbsəˌlutlɪ] 絕對地 adv.

❸ gorgeous [`gɔrdʒəs] 美麗動人的 adj.

❹ figure [`fɪgjɚ]（尤指女性的）身材 n.

❺ express [ɪk`sprɛs] 表達 v.

❻ political [pə`lɪtɪkl] 政治的 adj.

❼ impressive [ɪm`prɛsɪv] 令人印象深刻的 adj.

Is there a coffee shop where you like to spend your free time? Why do you like it?

你有喜歡度過空閒時間的咖啡店嗎？為什麼你喜歡它？

Yes, I often go to the coffee shop across the street from my office. It's called "Relaxing Time". There are some reasons that I like it. Its location is convenient for me, and the interior design is wonderful. Most importantly, the coffee there tastes great, which makes me relaxed when I spend my free time there.

是的，我常常去我辦公室對街的咖啡店。它叫做「放鬆時刻」。我喜歡它有一些理由。它的位置對我而言很便利，室內設計也很棒。最重要的是，那裡的咖啡很好喝，讓我在那裡度過空閒時間時很放鬆。

學習解析

❶ relaxing [rɪˋlæksɪŋ] 使人放鬆的 adj.

❷ location [loˋkeʃən] 地點 n.

❸ convenient [kənˋvinjənt] 便利的 adj.

❹ interior design 室內設計

致勝關鍵 KeyPoints

★台灣較知名的連鎖咖啡店：

英文	中文
Starbucks Coffee	星巴克
Louisa Coffee	路易莎
Dante Coffee	丹堤
Cama Coffee	Cama
Barista Coffee	西雅圖
Ikari Coffee	怡客
Mr. Brown Café	伯朗

最常考生
活主題 *3*

Pets 寵物

主題說明

近年來飼養寵物的人越來越多,因此這類有關於寵物的考題在考試中經常出現。考題通常會詢問個人經驗,例如是否有寵物,或者喜不喜歡某種動物。

常見問句句型

1. Do you have a ~?
   你有…嗎?

2. Do you like ~?
   你喜歡…嗎?

3. Are you afraid of ~?
   你怕…嗎?

4. Some people think ~. What is your opinion?
   有些人認為…。你的意見是什麼?

5. What kind of pet do you keep?
   你養什麼樣的寵物?

PART 2

常見回答句型

1. Yes, I have a ~.
   是的，我有…。

2. I don't like ~ because ~.
   我不喜歡…因為…。

3. Well, I'm afraid of ~. I think they are ~.
   嗯，我害怕…。我認為牠們…。

4. I totally agree with them. I think ~.
   我完全贊同他們的意見。我認為…。

5. Actually, I keep ~.
   事實上，我有養…。

 考題測試 >>>>

 答題示範 2-03.mp3

 模擬測驗 2-03-Q.mp3

這個部份共有十題。題目已事先錄音，每題經由耳機播出二次，不印在試卷上。第一至五題，每題回答時間 15 秒；第六至十題，每題回答時間 30 秒。每題播出後，請立即回答。回答時，不一定要用完整句子，但請在作答時間內盡量的表達。（可先聽答題示範音檔，再用模擬測驗音檔進行練習）

1 ## Are you afraid of any insects? What makes you afraid of them?

你怕任何昆蟲嗎？是什麼原因讓你害怕牠們？

 參考答案

Yes, I'm ❶scared of ants. It's ❷disgusting when they ❸gather around the food or drink I'm having.

有，我怕螞蟻。當他們聚集在我正在享用的食物或飲料周圍時，感覺很噁心。

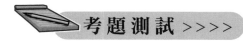

學習解析

❶ scared [skɛrd] 害怕的（口語） adj.

❷ disgusting [dɪs`gʌstɪŋ] 令人感覺噁心的 adj.

❸ gather [`gæðɚ] 聚集 v.

致勝關鍵 KeyPoints

　　本題問你是否怕任何昆蟲，只需要把你的感覺說出來，並說明理由即可。其他昆蟲還有：cockroaches 蟑螂、flies 蒼蠅、caterpillars 毛毛蟲。

Have you ever talked to your pet or any animal? If so, what did you say?

你曾經對你的寵物或任何動物說話嗎？如果有，你說什麼？

Yes, I talk to my dog. I say "good dog" and "catch it" almost every day. Although I don't know if he understands me, I ❶ can't help but keep talking to him.

是的，我會跟我的狗說話。我幾乎每天都會說「好狗狗」和「接住」。雖然我不知道他是否聽懂我說的話，但我就是忍不住一直對他說話。

學習解析

❶ can't help but 忍不住做…

致勝關鍵 KeyPoints

　　本題問是否曾經對寵物或動物說話，如果沒做過這件事的話，當然也可以回答沒有，例如：I don't think animals understand human languages, so I've never tried talking to them.（我不認為動物了解人類的語言，所以我從來沒試過對牠們說話）。

3 **Do you have a cat? What do you think about cats?**

你有貓嗎？你對貓的感覺如何？

 No. As a matter of fact, I don't like cats because they don't come when I call. However, some of my friends think that makes cats even cuter.

沒有，事實上，我不喜歡貓，因為我叫的時候牠們都不來。不過，我的一些朋友認為這樣讓貓更可愛了。

學習解析

❶ as a matter of fact 事實上

Do you have a pet? Tell me about it.

你有任何寵物嗎？告訴我關於牠的事。

 Yes, I have some ❶goldfish. They're very cute, and I feel relaxed when I watch them swimming. What's more, they're easy to feed.

有，我有一些金魚。牠們非常可愛，我在看牠們游泳時感到放鬆。而且，牠們很容易餵養。

學習解析

❶ goldfish [`gold,fɪʃ] 金魚 n.

 Do you have a dog? Why or why not? Tell me about your thoughts.

你有狗嗎？為什麼？告訴我你的想法。

 Actually, I haven't got any dogs. I really want a dog to play with, but my parents don't ❶allow me to keep one.

事實上，我沒有任何狗。我真的很想要一隻能一起玩的狗，但我爸媽不允許我養。

學習解析

❶ allow [ə`laʊ] 允許 v.

PART 2

6 Do you think it is acceptable to use animals for experiments? Tell me your opinion.

你認為使用動物進行實驗是可以接受的嗎？告訴我你的意見。

I think it's **cruel** and **unfair** to do so. I can't imagine how **hopeless** the animals feel. **Unfortunately**, animal testing is still allowed in most parts of the world, and every year there are still millions of animals that die in **labs**.

我認為這麼做很殘忍，而且不公平。我不能想像那些動物有多絕望。遺憾的是，動物試驗在世界上大部分的地方仍然是被允許的，每年仍然有數百萬的動物死在實驗室。

學習解析

❶ cruel [ˋkruəl] 殘忍的 adj.

❷ unfair [ʌnˋfɛr] 不公平的 adj.

❸ hopeless [ˋhoplɪs] 絕望的，沒有希望的 adj.

❹ unfortunately [ʌnˋfɔrtʃənɪtlɪ] 不幸地，遺憾地 adv.

❺ lab [læb] 實驗室（laboratory 的口語說法） n.

7 Have you ever had bad experiences with dogs? Tell me what happened.

你有對於狗的負面經驗嗎？告訴我發生了什麼事。

 I don't have such experience myself. However, one of my friends has been **bitten**❶ by a **stray**❷ dog. He thought he was going to die, but fortunately, it turned out that he was OK. After that, he is **extremely**❸ afraid of dogs, no matter how cute they are.

我自己沒有這種經驗。不過，我的一個朋友曾經被流浪狗咬過。他以為自己要死了，但幸運的是，結果他沒事。在那之後，他非常怕狗，不管牠們有多可愛。

學習解析

❶ bitten [`bɪtṇ] 咬（bite）的過去分詞
❷ stray [stre] 流浪的 adj.
❸ extremely [ɪk`strimlɪ] 極度地 adv.

致勝關鍵 KeyPoints

　　如果在 30 秒的題目中，遇到了自己沒有什麼相關經驗可說的情況，那麼不妨談談別人的經驗。例如本題，如果只說「不，我沒有這樣的經驗」就結束的話，肯定沒辦法拿高分。

PART 2

8 Should animals be kept in zoos? Tell me about your opinion.

動物應該被養在動物園裡嗎？告訴我你的意見。

I think a zoo is a great place to learn about the **behavior**❶ of animals, but it's also true that animals in zoos have lost their **freedom**❷. Therefore, I think there is no right answer to this question. If we could **communicate**❸ with animals, we might know how they really feel about living in a zoo.

我認為動物園是了解動物行為的好地方，但動物園中的動物失去了自由也是事實。所以，我認為這個問題沒有正確答案。要是我們能和動物溝通的話，或許就能知道他們對於在動物園生活的真實感受是什麼了。

學習解析

❶ behavior [bɪ`hevjɚ] 行為 n.

❷ freedom [`fridəm] 自由 n.

❸ communicate [kə`mjunə‚ket] 溝通 v.

致勝關鍵 KeyPoints

對於詢問意見的問題，有時候也可以採取中立的態度，並且分析正反兩面的論點。以本題為例，好處可以說 let people have more chances to be in touch with animals（讓人們有更多機會接觸動物），壞處可以說 there is not enough space for animals（動物沒有足夠的活動空間）。

9 What animal do you think is the funniest? What makes you think so?

你認為什麼動物最有趣？為什麼你這麼覺得？

 I like monkeys. I think they are the funniest because they act like humans, yet I can never expect what interesting things they will do next. Because of that, every time I go to a zoo, I always run to the area of monkeys first.

我喜歡猴子。我認為牠們是最有趣的，因為牠們行為像人一樣，但我永遠不能預測他們接下來會做什麼有趣的事。因為這個原因，每次我去動物園的時候，我總會先跑到猴子區。

學習解析

❶ monkey [`mʌŋkɪ] 猴子 n.
❷ funny [`fʌnɪ] 滑稽的，好笑的 adj.

致勝關鍵 KeyPoints

★問喜歡的動物時，可能採取的回答：

動物	英文	可能喜歡的原因
鯨魚	whale	they are huge and beautiful
狗	dog	they are cute and loyal to their owners
馬	horse	they can run very fast
鳥	bird	they can fly freely

Some people say that they don't like animals. What do you think may be the reason?

有些人說他們不喜歡動物。你認為原因可能是什麼？

 I don't think they really hate animals. Maybe they haven't tried to spend some time with animals, so they don't know how cute an animal can be. If they have a chance to play with dogs or cats, they will **definitely** fall in love with them.

我不認為他們真的討厭動物。或許他們沒有機會和動物度過一段時間，所以他們不知道動物可以有多可愛。如果他們有機會和狗或貓玩的話，他們一定會愛上牠們。

學習解析

❶ definitely [`dɛfənɪtlɪ] 確實地，絕對 adv.

School 學校生活

主題說明

不管你現在是不是學生，應該都經歷過學校的生活。本類考題多為「請你敘述一下你現在或過往的學生生活」，或是「你在學校中最喜歡的科目」、「你在學校中印象最深刻的老師」。

常見問句句型

1. What do you think are some qualities of ~?
   你認為…的特質是什麼？

2. What course would you ~?
   你會…什麼課程？

3. Do you ~ to school?
   你是…上學的嗎？

4. Some people think ~. What is your opinion?
   有些人認為…。你的意見是什麼？

5. Is it difficult to ~?
   …困難嗎？

常見回答句型

1. He/She has to be ~.
   他／她必須是…。

2. I would take ~ because ~.
   我會上…因為…。

3. Well, I usually ~ to school, but sometimes I ~.
   嗯，我通常…上學，但我有時候…。

4. I couldn't agree with them more. I think ~.
   我非常贊同他們的意見。我認為…。

5. As a matter of fact, I think ~.
   事實上，我認為…。

考題測試 >>>>

答題示範 🎧	模擬測驗 🎧
2-04.mp3	2-04-Q.mp3

這個部份共有十題。題目已事先錄音，每題經由耳機播出二次，不印在試卷上。第一至五題，每題回答時間 15 秒；第六至十題，每題回答時間 30 秒。每題播出後，請立即回答。回答時，不一定要用完整句子，但請在作答時間內盡量的表達。（可先聽答題示範音檔，再用模擬測驗音檔進行練習）

1 Do you ride a motorcycle to work or school? Why or why not?

你騎車上班或上學嗎？為什麼？

No, I don't ride a motorcycle. I think it's dangerous to ride it in heavy traffic. Actually, I always go to work on foot because my office is just 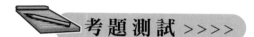around the corner from my home.

不，我不騎機車。我認為在繁忙的交通中騎機車很危險。事實上，我總是走路上班，因為我的辦公室就在我家附近。

Yes, I ride a motorcycle to work. Actually, I want a car, but I don't have enough money to buy one. That said, I think it's fast and ❸convenient enough to ride a motorcycle.

是的，我騎機車上班。其實我想要一輛車，但我沒有足夠的錢買車。話雖如此，我認為騎機車夠快也夠便利了。

學習解析

❶ on foot 用走路的方式
❷ around the corner 在附近
❸ convenient [kən`vinjənt] 便利的 adj.

2 Have you ever taken classes after school? Tell me about your experience.

你曾經在放學後上過課（補習）嗎？告訴我你的經驗。

I don't have such experience, but my ❶cousin David does. He is just an ❷elementary school student, but he learns a lot of stuff after school.

He always says he's tired of the classes, and he has no time to play.

我沒有這種經驗，但我的堂弟大衛有。他只是小學生，但他放學後學很多東西。他總是說自己對這些課感到厭倦，而且沒有時間玩耍。

PART 2

學習解析

❶ cousin [ˋkʌzn̩] 堂／表兄弟姊妹 n.

❷ elementary school student 小學生

3 Do you think it is difficult for people without a college degree to get a good job? Please explain.

你認為沒有大學學位的人會很難得到好工作嗎？請說明。

Yes, definitely. I think that's a basic **requirement**❶. Since most companies expect their employees to be college graduates, it's **harder**❷ **and harder** to find a good job without **higher education**❸.

是的，當然。我認為這是基本的必要條件。因為大部分的公司期望員工是大學畢業生，所以在沒有高等教育的情況下找到好工作越來越難。

Well, I think it **depends on**❹ what you mean by a good job. Many chefs haven't attended college, yet some of them earn more than doctors do.

嗯，我認為這取決於你所說的好工作是什麼意思。很多主廚沒上過大學，但其中有些人賺得比醫生還多。

學習解析

❶ requirement [rɪˋkwaɪrmənt] 必要條件 n.

❷ harder and harder 越來越難

❸ higher education 高等教育（大學以上）

❹ depend on 取決於…

142

Do you have some good tips to learn English? Tell me your experience.

你有一些學英語的好訣竅嗎？告訴我你的經驗。

 I listen to radio programs in English, and I think that improved my listening skills. Also, I attend a language school to get more opportunity to speak English.

我聽英語廣播節目，我認為那提升了我的聽力。我也上語言補習班以獲得更多說英語的機會。

學習解析

❶ improve [ɪm`pruv] 改善，增進 v.
❷ language school 語言補習班

致勝關鍵 KeyPoints

★本題問學好英文的祕訣，是英檢口說常考的主題。其他方法有：
Recite some good articles. 背誦好文章。
Memorize some new words every day. 每天記一些新單字。
Read *Time* magazine. 讀《時代》雜誌。
Make a foreign friend and have a language exchange with him/her.
結交外國友人並與他／她進行語言交換。

PART 2

5 What do you think are some qualities of a good student?

你認為好學生的一些特質是什麼？

 I think good students should be **hard-working** ❶ and **persistent** ❷.

Moreover, they know how to ask good questions to **clarify** ❸ their **doubts** ❹.

我認為好學生應該是努力而且堅持不懈的。而且，他們知道如何問好的問題來釐清疑惑。

學習解析

❶ hard-working [ˌhɑrd`wɝkɪŋ] 努力工作的，勤勉的 adj.

❷ persistent [pə`sɪstənt] 堅持不懈的 adj.

❸ clarify [`klærəˌfaɪ] 澄清，闡明 v.

❹ doubt [daʊt] 懷疑，疑問 n.

致勝關鍵 KeyPoints

★其他好學生的特質：

go to classes on time 準時上課

are always willing to learn 總是願意學習

try their best to solve difficult problems 盡全力解決困難的問題

6 What do you think are some qualities of a good teacher?

你認為好老師的一些特質是什麼？

 I think a good teacher should have ❶patience and good teaching skills. It is also important that they be kind to their students. In my opinion, since I find ❷textbooks hard to understand, I think teachers who can explain things in a simple way are the best.

我認為好老師應該要有耐心和好的教學能力。對待學生親切也很重要。就我看來，因為我覺得課本很難懂，所以我認為能用簡單的方式說明事情的老師是最好的。

學習解析

❶ patience [`peʃəns] 耐心 n.
❷ textbook [`tɛkstˌbʊk] 課本 n.

致勝關鍵 KeyPoints

★其他好老師的特質：

are never late to class 上課從不遲到

are nice to students and help them solve problems
對學生好並幫助他們解決問題

correct students' mistakes and explain what is wrong
糾正學生的錯誤並說明錯在哪裡

7 What is your favorite subject at school? Why do you like it? Tell me about it.

你在學校最喜愛的科目是什麼？為什麼喜歡？告訴我關於它的事。

 When it comes to my favorite subject, I think it must be English. I like it because my teacher has a **sense of humor** ❶ and teaches **grammar** ❷ in an interesting way. Therefore, most of my classmates and I do well in English, which makes us love English even more.

說到我最喜歡的科目，我想一定是英語。我喜歡英語是因為我的老師有幽默感，而且用有趣的方式教文法。所以，我和我大部分的同學英語表現都很好，這也使得我們更加喜愛英語。

學習解析

❶ sense of humor 幽默感
❷ grammar [ˋgræmɚ] 文法 n.

致勝關鍵 KeyPoints

★其他科目與喜歡的原因：

科目	英文	原因
數學	math	It's challenging to solve difficult math problems.
歷史	history	It's fun to know what happened in the past.
地理	geography	Knowing about different countries feels like traveling around the world.
科學	science	Doing experiments is fun.

Why is it sometimes very difficult for English learners to speak English? How can they improve?

為什麼英語學習者有時候很難說英語？他們可以怎樣改進？

The reason is that they don't practice very **frequently**❶. For those who have a lot of work to do, there isn't much time to practice. Even so, I think there are still many ways to improve. For example, they can listen to English **broadcasts**❷ on their way to work, or they can try **repeating**❸ interesting **dialogues**❹ in their favorite movies.

原因是他們不太常練習。對於有很多工作要做的人，沒有很多時間可以練習。即使如此，我想還是有很多改進的方法。舉例來說，他們可以在上班的路上聽英語廣播，或者可以試著複誦他們最愛的電影裡面有趣的對話。

學習解析

❶ frequently [`frikwəntlı] 頻繁地，經常地 adv.

❷ broadcast [`brɔdˌkæst] 廣播 n.

❸ repeat [rɪ`pit] 重複，複誦 v.

❹ dialogue [`daɪəˌlɔg] 對話 n.

致勝關鍵 KeyPoints

★除此之外，學英語的好處也是英檢常考的題目，幾個好處如下：

I can make good use of English publications.
我可以善用英語出版品。

I can travel by myself, not in a tour group.
我可以自助旅行不需跟團。

I can get the latest information in English.
我可以獲得最新的英語資訊。

I will have no difficulty communicating with foreign friends.
我將能毫無困難地與外國朋友溝通。

9 Would you consider studying abroad? Why or why not?

你會考慮在海外留學嗎？為什麼？

Yes, I hope I can study abroad. If I have a chance to do so, I can get to know people from different countries and learn about their cultures. However, I might give up the thought because of my financial situation. I'll have to take out a loan if I decide to study abroad, but I don't like being in debt.

是的，我希望我能在海外留學。如果我有機會留學的話，我可以認識來自不同國家的人，並且了解他們的文化。不過，我可能會因為我的財務狀況而放棄這個想法。如果我決定在海外留學，我必須貸款，但我不喜歡負債。

學習解析

❶ study abroad 在國外讀書，海外留學

❷ culture [ˋkʌltʃɚ] 文化 n.

❸ thought [θɔt] 想法 n.

❹ financial situation 財務狀況

❺ take out a loan 貸款

❻ in debt 負債的

10 Do you think schools should regulate what their students wear? Why or why not?

你認為學校應該管制學生的穿著嗎？為什麼？

 I don't think so. I think students should have the right to wear whatever they want. Just like we all have freedom of speech, I think students should also have the freedom to express themselves through what they wear. Also, they should be allowed to decide their own hairstyles, too.

我不認為。我認為學生應該有權利穿任何想穿的衣服。就像我們所有人都有言論自由一樣，我認為學生應該也有透過穿著表現自我的自由。還有，他們也應該被允許決定自己的髮型。

學習解析

❶ right [raɪt] 權利

❷ freedom of speech 言論自由

❸ express [ɪkˋsprɛs] 表達 v.

❹ hairstyle [ˋhɛrˌstaɪl] 髮型 n.

最常考生
活主題 *5*

Work & Jobs 工作

主題說明

不管你現在是不是上班族，相信現在或未來你都會經歷到工作的生活。本類考題多為「你是否喜歡你的工作」或是「你在工作場所中和主管、同事相處的情形」，以及「你理想的工作是什麼」等等。

常見問句句型

1. Do you get along with ~?
   你和…相處融洽嗎？

2. Do you like your ~?
   你喜歡你的…嗎？

3. Which is job is more ~, ~ or ~?
   哪種工作比較…，是…還是…？

4. Some people think ~. What is your opinion?
   有些人認為…。你的意見是什麼？

5. Are you satisfied with ~?
   你對…滿意嗎？

常見回答句型

1. I always get along with ~.
   我總是和…相處融洽。

2. I don't like ~ very much because ~.
   我不是很喜歡…因為…。

3. Well, in my opinion, I think being a ~ is more ~.
   嗯，在我看來，我認為當…比較…。

4. I don't agree with them at all. I believe ~.
   我一點也不同意他們。我相信…。

5. As a matter of fact, I'm not satisfied with ~.
   事實上，我對…不滿意。

 考 題 測 試 >>>>

 答題示範 2-05.mp3　模擬測驗 2-05-Q.mp3

這個部份共有十題。題目已事先錄音，每題經由耳機播出二次，不印在試卷上。第一至五題，每題回答時間 15 秒；第六至十題，每題回答時間 30 秒。每題播出後，請立即回答。回答時，不一定要用完整句子，但請在作答時間內盡量的表達。（可先聽答題示範音檔，再用模擬測驗音檔進行練習）

1 **How much salary do you think is reasonable for you? Have you reached the goal yet?**

你認為多少薪水對你而言是合理的？你達到這個目標了嗎？

❶The more, the better. Maybe fifty thousand dollars per month. To tell the truth, my ❷salary is not so good. I wonder when I'll get a ❸raise in my company.

越多越好。也許一個月五萬元吧。說實話，我的薪水沒有那麼好。我不知道什麼時候會在公司得到加薪。

學習解析

❶ the more, the better 越多越好

❷ salary [`sælərɪ] 薪水 n.

❸ raise [rez] 加薪 n.

2 ## What can you do to help your company be better in the future?

你可以做什麼讓你的公司在未來更好？

 I can ❶contribute what I have learned in school to my company. Also, I will try my best to ❷achieve the ❸objectives and ❹goals that my company has ❺set up.

我可以貢獻我在學校所學的給我的公司。我也會盡力達成公司所設定的目標。

❶ contribute [kən`trɪbjut] 貢獻 v.

❷ achieve [ə`tʃiv] 達成 v.

❸ objective [əb`dʒɛktɪv] 目標 n.

❹ goal [gol] 目標，終點 n.

❺ set up 建立

In your opinion, how many hours per week should people work?

在你看來，人們一週應該工作幾小時？

 According to the Labor Standard Act in Taiwan, we should not work more than 40 hours a week. Most people work 5 days a week, so that's 8 hours a day.

根據台灣的勞動基準法，我們每週不應該工作超過四十小時。大部分的人一週工作五天，所以是一天八小時。

學習解析

❶ according to 根據…
❷ Labor Standard Act 勞動基準法

 Do you get along with people who work together with you? Tell me your experience.

你跟和你一起工作的人相處融洽嗎？告訴我你的經驗。

 Yes. I like making friends, and I treat my colleagues like family, so I think it's not hard for me to get along with my coworkers.

是的。我喜歡交朋友，而且我對待同事就像家人一樣，所以我認為和同事相處融洽對我而言並不難。

學習解析

❶ make friends 交朋友

❷ colleague [ˋkɑlig] 同事 n.

致勝關鍵 KeyPoints

★和同事相處融洽的方法：

方法	英文
體貼	be considerate
知道其他人的興趣	know other people's interests
合作	cooperate
傾聽他人的問題	listen to other peoples' problems
請人吃晚餐	buy someone dinner
記得他人的生日	remember other people's birthdays

5 Do you like your current job? If not, what would your ideal job be like?

你喜歡目前的工作嗎？如果不喜歡的話，你理想的工作是什麼樣的？

 Yes, I like my ❶current job. It's just wonderful. Actually, I have been on my current job for a year. I'm familiar with what I do. Therefore, I'm not planning to change my job.

是的，我喜歡我目前的工作。它實在太棒了。事實上，我做我目前的工作一年了。我很熟悉我做的事。所以，我目前不打算換工作。

154

學習解析

❶ current [`kɝ·ənt] 目前的 adj.

致勝關鍵 KeyPoints

★理想工作的條件：

分類	英文	內容
工作	work/tasks	more challenging 更有挑戰性 full of variety 充滿變化 not too difficult 不會太困難
薪酬	compensation	high payment 高薪 good benefits 福利好 more days off 更多假日 insurance 保險 high year-end bonus 高年終獎金
環境	surrounding	non-smoking 禁菸的 independent space 獨立空間 perfect layout 完美的室內佈局
人際關係	relationship	get along with colleagues 與同事相處良好 nice and considerate supervisor 好心體貼的主管
位置	location	near my home 離家近 close to MRT stations 離捷運站近

PART 2

6 If your boss, manager, or teacher were very picky about what you do, how would you improve the situation?

假如你的老闆、經理或老師對於你所做的事非常挑剔，你會怎麼改善這個情況？

 Well, this is a tough question. Maybe it's just because my boss doesn't understand the way I do my job. I think I would try to ❶communicate with him and let him know what I have achieved.

However, if that doesn't work, I might consider finding a new job.
嗯，這是很難的問題。或許那只是因為我的老闆不了解我工作的方式。我想我會試圖和他溝通，並且讓他知道我達成的事情。不過，如果那樣沒用的話，我可能會考慮找新的工作。

學習解析

❶ communicate [kəˋmjunəˌket] 溝通 v.

7 Would you like to be a manager or supervisor? Why or why not?

你想成為一位經理或是主管嗎？為什麼？

 No, I don't want to be a ❶leader. I think I'll feel a lot of ❷pressure. I don't want to have too much ❸workload, and I think it's important to have some time to relax and enjoy ❹leisure activities. I don't think that would be possible if I became a manager or ❺supervisor.
不，我不想當領導人。我想我會感覺很有壓力。我不想要有太多工作量，而

156

且我認為有一些時間放鬆並且享受休閒活動很重要。如果我成為經理或主管，我想那就不可能了。

學習解析

❶ leader [`lidə`] 領導者 n.

❷ pressure [`prɛʃə`] 壓力 n.

❸ workload [`wɜk͵lod] 工作量 n.

❹ leisure activity 休閒活動

❺ supervisor [`supə͵vaɪzə`] 主管 n.

8 In your opinion, which of the following jobs is more interesting, a doctor or an artist? Why do you think so?

在你看來，以下哪種工作比較有趣，是醫師還是藝術家？為什麼你這麼認為？

I think it is more interesting to be an ❶artist. Artists always try to create new things, so their life must be full of ❷possibilities. However, many people ❸would rather become doctors to get higher and more ❹stable ❺income. No wonder my parents always want me to apply to a ❻medical school.

我認為當藝術家比較有趣。藝術家總是試圖創造新的東西，所以他們的生活一定充滿了可能性。不過，很多人寧願當醫師以獲得更高、更穩定的收入。難怪我爸媽總是希望我報名醫學院。

PART 2

學習解析

❶ artist [`ɑrtɪst] 藝術家 n.

❷ possibility [ˌpɑsə`bɪlətɪ] 可能性 n.

❸ would rather 寧願…

❹ stable [`stebl] 穩定的 adj.

❺ income [`ɪn͵kʌm] 收入 n.

❻ medical school 醫學院

9 **In your opinion, which of the following jobs is more dangerous, a firefighter or a soldier? Why do you think so?**

在你看來，以下哪種工作比較危險，是消防員還是軍人？為什麼你這麼認為？

 Since there is no war right now, I think firefighters face more risks than soldiers do. There are thousands of home fires in Taiwan every year, and firefighters sometimes run into houses on fire in order to save people inside. There are some firefighters who died while on duty, proving that their job is dangerous.

因為現在沒有戰爭，所以我認為消防員面臨的風險比軍人多。台灣每年有成千上萬件住宅火災，而消防員有時候會為了救裡面的人而跑進著火的房子。有一些消防員在執勤時死亡，證明他們的工作很危險。

學習解析

❶ firefighter [`faɪr͵faɪtɚ] 消防員 n.

❷ soldier [`soldʒɚ] 士兵 n.

❸ on duty 值勤中

致勝關鍵 KeyPoints

★其他危險性高的職業：

中文	英文
戰地記者	war journalist
特技演員	stuntman/stuntwoman
間諜	spy / secret agent

10 If you constantly had more workload than your colleagues did, what would you do?

如果你的工作量總是比同事多，你會怎麼做？

Oh, that's just not acceptable❶. I would be very upset. I think I would try to solve❷ the problem by communicating with them. I'd suppose❸ that they didn't notice the problem and would try to improve the situation after we talk about it. If that doesn't work, I will try to find a new job.

噢，那簡直不能接受。我會很生氣。我想我會試圖藉由和他們溝通來解決這個問題。我會假設他們沒有注意到這個問題，在我們談過之後就會試圖改善狀況。如果那樣沒有用的話，我會試著找新的工作。

學習解析

❶ acceptable [ək`sɛptəbl] 可以接受的 adj.

❷ solve [sɑlv] 解決 v.

❸ suppose [sə`poz] 假設 v.

159

最常考生
活主題 6

Movies & Internet 電影與網路

主題說明

電影與網際網路已經成為現代生活中不可欠缺的一部分。本類常見考題有「你喜歡什麼樣的電影」、「你通常去電影院或者用串流服務看電影」、「你每天花在網路上的時間有多少」等等。

常見問句句型

1. How often do you ~?
   你多常…？

2. Do you like ~?
   你喜歡…嗎？

3. What type of ~ do you like?
   你喜歡什麼類型的…？

4. How much time do you spend ~?
   你花多少時間…？

5. Do you ~ on the Internet?
   你會在網路上…嗎？

常見回答句型

1. I ~ once a week / twice a month / several times a year.
   我…一週一次／一個月兩次／一年數次。

2. I don't like ~ so much because ~.
   我不是很喜歡…因為…。

3. Actually, I like ~ because ~.
   事實上，我喜歡…因為…。

4. I spend ~ on ~ per day.
   我每天在…上花（時間）。

5. As a matter of fact, I usually ~ on the Internet.
   事實上，我通常會在網路上…。

 考題測試 >>>>

答題示範 🎧 2-06.mp3　　模擬測驗 🎧 2-06-Q.mp3

這個部份共有十題。題目已事先錄音，每題經由耳機播出二次，不印在試卷上。第一至五題，每題回答時間 15 秒；第六至十題，每題回答時間 30 秒。每題播出後，請立即回答。回答時，不一定要用完整句子，但請在作答時間內盡量的表達。（可先聽答題示範音檔，再用模擬測驗音檔進行練習）

 ### How often do you go to the movies? When do you usually go to a movie?

你多常去電影院看電影？你通常什麼時候去看電影？

參考答案

I go to the movies twice a month. If there's a really great movie, I'll go for it immediately. Sometimes I go to a movie when I hang out with my friends.

我一個月去電影院看電影兩次。如果有真的很好的電影，我會馬上去看。有時候我會在和朋友一起玩的時候去電影院看電影。

學習解析

❶ twice [twaɪs] 兩次 adv.

❷ Immediately [ɪ`midɪɪtlɪ] 立刻，馬上

❸ hang out （和朋友）在某個地方消磨時間

致勝關鍵 KeyPoints

★頻率的英文說法：

中文	英文
總是	always
幾乎總是	nearly always
通常	usually
經常	frequently
有時候	sometimes
不常	not often
偶爾	once in a while
很少	seldom
幾乎不曾	hardly ever
從未	never
一個月超過三次	over three times a month

Have you ever tried to build a website? Tell me about your experience.

你曾經試過架設網站嗎？告訴我你的經驗。

 No, I have never made a website myself. I'm not a famous person, so I don't think I need a website to promote myself. Besides, I don't know how to make a website.

不，我自己從來沒有做過網站。我不是有名的人，所以我不認為自己需要網站來宣傳自己。而且，我不知道要怎麼做一個網站。

學習解析

❶ website [`wɛb͵saɪt] 網站 n.

❷ promote [prə`mot] 宣傳 v.

 How much do you pay for your cell phone bill every month? Do you think that's too much?

你每個月花多少錢在手機帳單上？你覺得太多了嗎？

 I spend 800 dollars per month for unlimited data, and I think the fee's quite high. I don't spend much time using my phone, so maybe I should go for a cheaper data plan.

我每個月為了上網吃到飽花八百元，我認為費用挺高的。我不會花很多時間使用手機，所以或許我應該選擇比較便宜的行動上網方案。

學習解析

❶ unlimited data 上網吃到飽（無限的行動上網數據量）

163

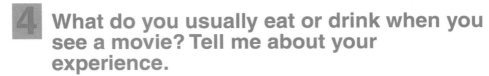

❷ data plan 行動上網方案（行動上網數據量的方案）

4 What do you usually eat or drink when you see a movie? Tell me about your experience.

你在電影院看電影時通常吃或喝什麼？告訴我你的經驗。

I eat **popcorn**❶ and drink **coke**❷, but not often. Actually, I'm afraid of being too loud while eating or drinking because people around me may feel **annoyed**❸.

我吃爆米花、喝可樂，但是不常。事實上，我怕吃或喝東西時太大聲，因為我周圍的人可能會覺得生氣。

學習解析

❶ popcorn [`pɑpˌkɔrn] 爆米花 n.

❷ coke [kok] 可樂 n.

❸ annoyed [ə`nɔɪd] 被惹惱的 adj.

致勝關鍵 KeyPoints

★其他常帶進電影院的零食：

中文	英文
炸雞	fried chicken
滷味	braised food
洋芋片	potato chips
熱狗堡	hot dog

Do you listen to movie soundtracks after seeing a movie? What is your favorite soundtrack?

你看電影之後會聽電影配樂（原聲帶）嗎？你最喜歡的配樂是什麼？

 Yes. When I listen to movie **soundtracks**, it feels like I'm in that movie. My favorite soundtrack is "My Heart Will Go On" in "Titanic". The song is really beautiful.

會。當我聽電影配樂的時候，感覺就像置身於電影之中。我最愛的配樂是《鐵達尼號》裡的〈My Heart Will Go On〉。這首歌真的很美。

學習解析

❶ soundtrack [`saʊndˌtræk]（電影）配樂，原聲帶 n.

致勝關鍵 KeyPoints

★其他配樂優秀的知名電影：

中文	英文
全面啟動	Inception
樂來樂愛你	La La Land
一個巨星的誕生	A Star is Born
冰雪奇緣	Frozen
社群網戰	The Social Network

★看電影的說法：

英文	中文
go to the movies	去電影院看電影（表示一種活動，而不特指某部電影）
go to a movie	去電影院看一部電影
see a movie	在電影院看一部電影
watch a movie	用電視或電腦螢幕看一部電影

6 How much time do you spend on your smartphone each day? When do you usually use it?

你每天花多少時間在你的智慧型手機上？你通常什麼時候使用它？

I spend around five hours on my ❶smartphone per day. I check Facebook and Instagram ❷first thing in the morning when the alarm ❸goes off, and I ❹stick to my phone on the bus, during my lunch break, and before bed. I think I should reduce the time I use it because I find it hard to ❺focus on other things.

我每天花大約五個小時在智慧型手機上。我在早上鬧鐘響的時候就馬上查看 Facebook 和 Instagram，而我在公車上、午餐休息時、上床睡覺前都會黏著手機。我想我應該減少使用手機的時間，因為我發現很難專注在其他事情上。

學習解析

❶ smartphone [`smɑrt͵fon] 智慧型手機 n.

❷ first thing in the morning 早上一起來就…

❸ go off （鬧鐘）響起

❹ stick to 堅持，忠於…

❺ focus on 專注於…

7 Do you prefer to watch a movie via a streaming service or go to a theater? Please explain your choice.

你比較喜歡透過串流服務看電影還是去電影院？請說明你的選擇。

Although it's ❶convenient to watch movies online, I still prefer to go to a theater. In a theater, there are ❷surround sound speakers and huge screens, which make ❸action movies more exciting. Also, many movie theaters have ❹food courts, so after seeing a movie, I can have a meal there with my friends.

雖然在網路上看電影很便利，但我還是偏好去電影院看電影。在電影院有環繞音響和大型銀幕，讓動作電影更刺激。還有，許多電影院有美食街，所以看完電影之後，我可以和我的朋友在那裡用餐。

學習解析

❶ convenient [kən`vinjənt] 便利的 adj.

❷ surround sound speakers 環繞音響

❸ action movie 動作電影

❹ food court 商場的美食街

致勝關鍵 KeyPoints

★去戲院的好處：

中文	英文
大螢幕	big screen
音響效果好	good sound effect
與朋友相聚	get together with friends
看到最新的電影	see the latest movies

★在網路上看電影的好處：

中文	英文
待在家中	stay at home
便宜	inexpensive
在任何時候重看	watch again anytime
不用排隊	no need to wait in line
隨時暫停	pause anytime
看字幕學英文	learn English from subtitles

8 Do you like online shopping? Why or why not?

你喜歡網路購物嗎？為什麼？

 Yes, I like online shopping. I think it's very convenient, especially when the thing I want to buy is hard to find in stores nearby. It also saves the time and ❶transportation cost of going to a store far away.

回 答 問 題

That said, some are still **concerned** about the **security** of their
personal information.

是的，我喜歡網路購物。我認為它非常便利，尤其是我想要買的東西在附近的店很難找到的時候。它也能節省去遙遠的商店的時間和交通費用。話雖如此，有些人還是擔心個人資訊的安全性。

學習解析

❶ transportation [ˌtrænspəˈteʃən] 交通運輸 n.
❷ concerned [kənˈsɝnd] 擔心的 adj.
❸ security [sɪˈkjʊrətɪ] 安全 n.
❹ personal information 個人資訊

---

9 Do you spend money in mobile games? Do you think it's worth it?

你會在手機遊戲裡花錢嗎？你認為值得嗎？

Yes, I buy **items** in a game so I have a better chance to **defeat** other players. Recently, however, I **realized** that in order to keep winning, I have to keep spending money in the game. I feel that my **achievements** in the game mean nothing in the real world, so I'm considering quitting it.

會，我會買遊戲裡的道具，讓我有比較好的機率打敗其他玩家。不過，最近我了解到，為了繼續贏下去，我必須持續在這個遊戲裡花錢。我感覺自己遊戲裡的成就在現實生活沒有意義，所以我正在考慮放棄不玩。

PART 2

學習解析

❶ item [`aɪtəm] 物品，（遊戲裡的）道具 n.

❷ defeat [dɪ`fit] 打敗 v.

❸ realize [`rɪəˌlaɪz] 了解到… v.

❹ achievement [ə`tʃivmənt] 成就 n.

10 **For what do you use an email service? Tell me about your experience.**

你為了什麼而使用電子郵件服務？告訴我你的經驗。

 I send and receive emails for work. Since many of my **clients**❶ live in foreign countries, most of the time we communicate by email. I do it every day, and it has become an important part of my daily **routine**❷. The only problem is that I receive a lot of **spam**❸, making it more difficult to find important messages.

我為了工作而收發電子郵件。因為我很多客戶住在國外，所以我們大多用電子郵件溝通。我每天都做這件事，它成為了我每天例行公事很重要的一部分。唯一的問題是我收到很多垃圾郵件，使得我比較難找到重要的訊息。

學習解析

❶ clilent [`klaɪənt] 客戶 n.

❷ routine [ru`tin] 例行公事 n.

❸ spam [spæm] 垃圾郵件 n.

最常考生
活主題 *7*

Shopping 購物

主題說明

每個人都有購物的經驗，因此購物也成為必考主題之一，本類常見題目有「你喜歡什麼樣的購物方式」、「你通常多久購物一次」，或者用 where 詢問「你通常在哪裡購物。

常見問句句型

1. Where do you usually buy ~?
   你通常在哪裡買…？

2. Do you like to ~ in ~?
   你喜歡在…做…嗎？

3. How often do you ~?
   你多常…？

4. Have you ever ~?
   你曾經…嗎？

5. Do you ~ when you ~?
   當你…的時候，你會…嗎？

常見回答句型

1. I often buy ~ in ~.
   我常常在…買…。

2. I don't like ~ so much because ~.
   我不是很喜歡…因為…。

3. I ~ once in a while.
   我偶爾…。

4. No, I have never ~.
   不，我從來不曾…。

5. Yes, I usually ~.
   是的，我通常…。

考 題 測 試 >>>>

答題示範
2-07.mp3

模擬測驗
2-07-Q.mp3

這個部份共有十題。題目已事先錄音，每題經由耳機播出二次，不印在試卷上。第一至五題，每題回答時間 15 秒；第六至十題，每題回答時間 30 秒。每題播出後，請立即回答。回答時，不一定要用完整句子，但請在作答時間內盡量的表達。（可先聽答題示範音檔，再用模擬測驗音檔進行練習）

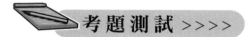 **What items do you buy most often? Tell me about your experience.**

你最常買的物品是什麼？告訴我你的經驗。

 Most of the time I go shopping for clothes because I want to keep up❶ with fashion trends❷. I also like to shop for beauty products with my friends.

大多數的時候我逛街買衣服，因為我想要跟上時尚趨勢。我也喜歡跟朋友一起採買美容產品。

學習解析

❶ keep up with 跟上⋯
❷ trend [trɛnd] 趨勢 n.

致勝關鍵 KeyPoints

★購買物品的種類：

中文	英文
書	books
文具	stationery
化妝品	cosmetics
保養品	skincare products
（穿戴的）配件	accessories
電腦周邊	computer accessories
食品雜貨	groceries
家電	home appliances

Where do you like to shop for clothes? Why do you like that place?

你喜歡在哪裡採購衣服？為什麼你喜歡那裡？

I usually go to SOGO Department Store ❶ because it has all kinds of brands ❷. However, I also find myself shopping online more often recently. I can see many items online without going here and there.
我通常去 SOGO 百貨公司,因為那裡有各種品牌。不過,我也發現自己最近更常在網路上購物。我在網路上不用到處跑就能看到許多品項。

學習解析

❶ department store 百貨公司
❷ brand [brænd] 品牌 n.

3 ## What kind of gift would you buy for Mother's Day? Please explain your choice.

你會為了母親節買什麼樣的禮物?請說明你的選擇。

 I would buy some herbal tea ❶ for my mom. She makes it a habit to ❷ drink herbal tea every day because she thinks it's good for health. Therefore, I think my mom would like it.
我會買一些草本茶給我媽媽。她習慣每天喝草本茶,因為她認為草本茶對健康很好。所以我認為我媽媽會喜歡。

學習解析

❶ herbal tea 草本茶
❷ make it a habit to 習慣做⋯(維持做⋯的習慣)

致勝關鍵 KeyPoints

★購買物品的地方：

中文	英文
文具店	stationery shop
精品店	boutique
購物中心	shopping mall

4 Do you prefer to pay in cash or by credit card? Please explain your choice.

你比較喜歡用現金還是信用卡付款？請說明你的選擇。

參考答案 I prefer to use a credit card. With a credit card, I don't need to worry about whether I have enough cash. Besides, there are usually special offers just for those who pay by card.

我比較喜歡使用信用卡。有了信用卡，我就不需要擔心是否有足夠的現金。而且，通常也會有只提供給刷卡付款者的特別優惠。

學習解析

❶ credit card 信用卡
❷ special offer 特別優惠

PART 2

 Have you ever returned something you bought? Tell me about your experience.

你曾經退過你買的東西嗎？告訴我你的經驗。

 No, I haven't, but I have exchanged❶ a pair of jeans for another size. I bought them without trying them on❷, and they turned out to❸ be too tight for me, so I had to exchange them.

不，我沒有，但我曾經把一條牛仔褲換成別的尺寸。我沒試穿就買了，結果對我來說太緊，所以我不得不換貨。

學習解析

❶ exchange [ɪksˋtʃendʒ] 交換 v.

❷ try on 試穿…

❸ turn out to 結果…

 Do you buy more things during sales? Why or why not?

特賣活動期間你會買比較多的東西嗎？為什麼？

 Definitely. Most stuff gets cheaper during sales, so I can get more with the same amount❶ of money. By the way, around some holidays, such as Mother's Day and Christmas, there are usually better deals❷, and I would take the chance to buy better gifts for my loved ones.

當然。大部分的東西在特賣時都變得比較便宜，所以我可以用同樣多的錢買到更多東西。對了，在一些節日前後，例如母親節和聖誕節，通常會有比較划算的價格，而我會利用機會為我所愛的人買比較好的禮物。

176

學習解析

❶ amount [ə`maʊnt] 總額，數量 n.
❷ deal [dil] 划算的交易、價格 n.

致勝關鍵 KeyPoints

★特賣活動的種類：

中文	英文
開幕特賣	opening sale
結束營業特賣	closing down sale
季末特賣	end of season sale
夏季特賣	summer sale
冬季特賣	winter sale

7 Have you ever bought used items? Why did you buy them instead of new ones?

你買過二手的東西嗎？你為什麼買二手貨而不是買新的？

Yes, I sometimes buy used books because they are cheaper. Many used books are just like new ones, so I think they're great ❶bargains. However, I wouldn't buy ❷electronic devices that have been used because they get ❸out of order easily. No matter how low the price might be, I wouldn't buy something that could become totally ❹useless in the future.

是的，我有時候會買二手書，因為它們比較便宜。許多二手書看起來就像新的一樣，所以我認為它們非常划算。不過，我不會買被用過的電子設備，因為它們很容易故障。不管價格可能有多低，我都不會買未來可能變得完全沒用的東西。

學習解析

❶ bargain [`bɑrgɪn] 划算、便宜的東西 n.

❷ electronic device 電子設備

❸ out of order 故障的

❹ useless [`juslɪs] 沒用的 adj.

8 Do you make a list before you go shopping? Why or why not?

你去購物之前會列出清單嗎？為什麼？

No, I think it's a waste of time. When I go shopping in a supermarket, I always find something I haven't thought of ❶ and decide to buy it immediately ❷, so it's not very helpful to make a shopping list in advance ❸. However, my mother does make shopping lists because she usually forgets what to buy.

不，我認為那是浪費時間。當我在超市購物的時候，我總是會發現我沒想過的東西，並且立刻決定買下，所以事先做購物清單不是很有幫助。不過，我媽媽會做購物清單，因為她通常會忘記要買什麼。

學習解析

❶ think of 想到…

❷ immediately [ɪ`midɪɪtlɪ] 立即，馬上

❸ in advance 事先

9 Have you ever bought a video game? Tell me about your experience. If you haven't, would you like to?

你買過電玩遊戲嗎？告訴我你的經驗。如果沒有的話，你想買嗎？

Yes, I have bought some games for my Nintendo Switch. Actually, I bought the games on Nintendo's online shop. It is very convenient❶ because I can pay by card and download❷ the games immediately. ❸Unfortunately, I have a lot of work to do these days and don't have so much free time to play the games.

是的，我為我的任天堂 Switch 買過一些遊戲。事實上，我是在任天堂的網路商店買那些遊戲的。那非常方便，因為我可以用信用卡付款，並且立刻下載遊戲。遺憾的是，我最近有很多工作要做，沒有很多空閒時間玩那些遊戲。

學習解析

❶ convenient [kən`vinjənt] 方便的 adj.

❷ download [`daʊnˌlod] 下載 v.

❸ unfortunately [ʌn`fɔrtʃənɪtlɪ] 不幸地，遺憾地 adv.

PART 2

10 What is the most expensive thing you have bought? Why did you buy it? Tell me about it.

你買過最貴的東西是什麼？你為什麼買它？告訴我關於它的事。

I bought a Macbook two years ago. It cost me about 40,000 dollars, and I kept saving money for a year before buying it. I bought it because I was planning to start my YouTube channel, and I needed a good computer to edit❶ my videos. Its performance❷ is still good now, and I don't regret❸ buying it.

我兩年前買了 Macbook。那花了我大約 40,000 元，我在買之前持續存了一年的錢。我買它是因為我當時打算開設 YouTube 頻道，而我需要好的電腦來編輯影片。它的性能現在還是很好，我不後悔買它。

學習解析

❶ edit [`ɛdɪt] 編輯 v.

❷ performance [pə`fɔrməns] 性能 n.

❸ regret [rɪ`grɛt] 後悔 v.

最常考生
活主題 *8*

Weather 天氣

主題說明

「天氣」是外國人最喜歡談論的話題之一，因此也成為英檢考試題目的常考主題。常見的題目有「你喜歡怎樣的天氣」、「你在陰天時感覺如何」等等，不會有艱澀的專業內容。

常 見 問 句 句 型

1. Do you like ~?
   你喜歡…嗎？

2. Do you often ~ on ~ days?
   你常在…的日子…嗎？

3. Have you ever ~ on ~ days?
   你曾經在…的日子…嗎？

4. What do you think about ~?
   你對於…有什麼想法？

5. Would you ~ if ~?
   如果…的話，你會…嗎？

PART 2

常見回答句型

1. I like ~ very much because ~.
   我很喜歡…因為…。

2. No, I seldom ~ on ~ days.
   不，我很少在…的日子…。

3. Actually, I have never ~.
   事實上，我從來不曾…。

4. I think that ~.
   我認為…。

5. No, I wouldn't ~.
   不，我不會…。

考 題 測 試 >>>>

答題示範 🎧 2-08.mp3　　模擬測驗 🎧 2-08-Q.mp3

這個部份共有十題。題目已事先錄音，每題經由耳機播出二次，不印在試卷上。第一至五題，每題回答時間 15 秒；第六至十題，每題回答時間 30 秒。每題播出後，請立即回答。回答時，不一定要用完整句子，但請在作答時間內盡量的表達。（可先聽答題示範音檔，再用模擬測驗音檔進行練習）

1 ## What kind of weather do you like? Why do you like it?

你喜歡怎樣的天氣？為什麼？

參考答案

I like hot and sunny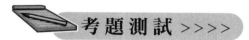 weather. Hanging around in shorts and a T-shirt under the sun is more comfortable than wearing a lot of clothes to stay warm on cold days.

我喜歡炎熱而晴朗的天氣。在太陽下穿著短褲和 T 恤閒逛，比在寒冷的日子穿很多衣服保持溫暖來得舒適。

學習解析

❶ sunny [`sʌnɪ] 晴朗的 adj.

❷ hang around 閒逛

❸ shorts [ʃɔrts] 短褲 n.

❹ comfortable [`kʌmfɚtəbḷ] 使人舒服的 adj.

致勝關鍵 KeyPoints

★天氣的英文說法：

英文	中文	英文	中文
sunny	晴朗的	snow storm	暴風雪
cloudy	多雲的，陰天的	thunder storm	雷陣雨
foggy	多霧的	mild climate	溫和的氣候
rainy	下雨的	typhoon	颱風

2 What is the ideal weather for swimming at the beach? Why do you think so?

在海邊游泳的理想天氣是什麼？你為什麼這麼認為？

 I think it's best to swim at the beach on sunny days. The sea is usually calmer❶ on sunny days, making it safer to swim. The beach

PART 2

also looks more beautiful under the blue sky.

我認為晴天在海邊游泳是最好的。晴天時海通常比較平靜,所以游泳比較安全。海灘在藍天之下看起來也比較美。

學習解析

❶ calm [kɑm] 平靜的 adj.

3 What kind of weather makes you sad? Why do you think so?

怎樣的天氣讓你難過?為什麼你這麼認為?

  ❶Rainy days and ❷cloudy days. I don't like them because they make me ❸sleepy and tired of everything. I think that's because we need ❹sunlight to feel ❺energetic and healthy.

雨天和陰天。我不喜歡這樣的日子,因為會讓我想睡,而且對每件事都感到厭倦。我想那是因為我們需要陽光來感覺有活力而健康。

學習解析

❶ rainy [`renɪ] 下雨的 adj.

❷ cloudy [`klaʊdɪ] 多雲的,陰天的 adj.

❸ sleepy [`slipɪ] 想睡的 adj.

❹ sunlight [`sʌn͵laɪt] 陽光 n.

❺ energetic [͵ɛnɚ`dʒɛtɪk] 充滿活力的 adj.

Do you check weather forecasts every day? Why or why not?

你每天查看氣象預報嗎？為什麼？

 I ❶used to, but now I only do it once in a while because I don't trust ❷weather forecasts anymore. They are sometimes wrong, and I may make wrong decisions if I ❸totally believe them.

我以前會，但現在我只會偶爾看，因為我不再相信氣象預報了。氣象預報有時候是錯的，如果我完全相信的話就有可能做出錯誤的決定。

學習解析

❶ used to 以前慣於做…

❷ weather forecast 氣象預報

❸ totally [`totḷɪ] 完全地 adv.

 Do you prefer to stay at home on rainy days? Why or why not?

下雨天你比較喜歡待在家嗎？為什麼？

 Yes, I always stay at home when it's raining. I don't like it when my shoes get wet in the rain, so I think I'm ❶better off reading novels or playing games at home.

是的，下雨時我總是待在家裡。我不喜歡鞋子在雨中濕掉，所以我認為我還是在家讀小說或玩遊戲比較好。

學習解析

❶ better off 情況比較好

6 How can we prepare for an earthquake? Do you think you are well-prepared?

我們可以怎樣為地震做準備？你認為你準備充足嗎？

參考答案

We can prepare emergency❶ supplies❷ ahead of time❸. For example, we can prepare some water and food in case we get trapped❹ after an earthquake❺. It's also important to have a whistle❻ so rescue teams❼ can hear us. However, I have to admit that I haven't prepared an emergency kit❽ yet.

我們可以提前準備緊急用品。舉例來說，我們可以準備一些水和食物，以防萬一我們在地震後被困住。有口哨讓救援隊能聽到我們也很重要。不過，我必須承認自己還沒準備應急用品包。

學習解析

❶ emergency [ɪˋmɝdʒənsɪ] 緊急情況 n.

❷ supply [səˋplaɪ] 用品 n.

❸ ahead of time 提前

❹ trapped [træpt] 受困的 adj.

❺ earthquake [ˋɝθ͵kwek] 地震 n.

❻ whistle [ˋhwɪsl̩] 口哨 n.

❼ rescue team 救援隊

❽ kit [kɪt] 成套用具組 n.

致勝關鍵 KeyPoints

★自然災害的英文說法：

英文	中文
typhoon	颱風
tornado	龍捲風
earthquake	地震
flood	洪水
landslide	山崩
volcanic eruption	火山爆發
snow storm	暴風雪

7 What kind of weather do you think is good for studying? Why do you think so?

你認為什麼樣的天氣適合學習？為什麼你這麼認為？

I think it's best to study on rainy days. On rainy days, I prefer to stay at home and not to go out, so I will have a lot of free time. In order to kill time, I will spend more time on my schoolwork❶. Also, the sound of rain also makes it easier to concentrate❷ when studying.

我認為在雨天學習是最好的。在雨天，我比較喜歡待在家不要出門，所以我會有很多空閒時間。為了殺時間，我會花比較多的時間在作業上。還有，下雨的聲音也讓人在學習時比較容易專注。

PART 2

學習解析

❶ schoolwork [`skul͵wɝk] 學校或課堂上的作業 n.

❷ concentrate [`kɑnsən͵tret] 專注 v.

8 Do you think it is necessary that the government declare a typhoon holiday? Why or why not?

你認為政府有必要宣布颱風假嗎？為什麼？

 Of course it's necessary. If the government doesn't do so, some companies may force their employees to go to work during a storm. Even though companies may lose money if they let their employees have a day off, I think safety is still more important than anything else.

當然有必要。如果政府不這麼做的話，有些公司可能強迫員工在暴風雨時期上班。儘管公司讓員工休假的話可能會損失錢，但我認為安全仍然比其他事都重要。

學習解析

❶ necessary [`nɛsə͵sɛrɪ] 必要的 adj.

❷ government [`gʌvɚnmənt] 政府 n.

❸ force [fors] 強迫 v.

❹ storm [stɔrm] 暴風雨 n.

Have you ever seen snow before? If you haven't, would you like to?

你以前看過雪嗎？如果沒有的話，你想看嗎？

Yes, I have seen it before. It was a wonderful experience, and I can't forget what I saw. It was when I visited Kyoto in winter three years ago. The old houses and temples were covered with snow, which makes the city even more beautiful. I hope I will have a chance to see that again.

是的，我以前看過雪。那是很棒的經驗，我忘不了我所看到的。那是我三年前在冬天拜訪京都的時候。老房子和寺廟覆蓋著雪，讓這個城市更加美麗。我希望我有機會再看一次。

學習解析

❶ experience [ɪk`spɪrɪəns] 經驗 n.
❷ temple [`tɛmpl] 寺廟 n.
❸ cover [`kʌvɚ] 覆蓋 v.

Have you ever experienced a flood? If you haven't, please describe the floods you have seen in the media.

你經歷過水災嗎？如果沒有的話，請描述你在媒體中看過的水災。

I have experienced a big flood when I was ten years old. Typhoon Nari hit Taipei and brought a lot of rain, and many places were flooded, including Taipei Train Station and some MRT stations. It was a terrible disaster❷, and I hope I will not experience it again.

我在十歲的時候經歷過一場大水災。納莉颱風侵襲台北,帶來許多降雨,很多地方淹水了,包括台北車站和一些捷運站。那是很糟糕的災害,我希望我不會再經歷一次。

學習解析

❶ flood [flʌd] 水災 n. 淹沒 v.

❷ disaster [dɪ`zæstɚ] 災害 n.

最常考生
活主題 9

English Learning 英語學習

主題說明

「學習英語」是很基本且常考的話題。常見的問題有「你為什麼學英語」、「台灣為什麼有許多語言補習班」等，而「你學英語多久了」這個問題也曾多次出現。

常見問句句型

1. **Why do you learn English?**
   你為什麼學英語？

2. **How long have you been ~?**
   你…多久了？

3. **What may be the reasons that ~?**
   …的原因可能是什麼？

4. **Can you share some tips on how to ~?**
   你可以分享一些如何…的祕訣嗎？

5. **Would you ~ if ~?**
   如果…的話，你會…嗎？

常見回答句型

1. I learn English because ~.

   我因為…而學習英語。

2. I've been ~ for ~.

   我已經…有…（時間）了。

3. Actually, I have no idea why ~. Maybe it's because ~.

   事實上，我不知道為什麼…。或許是因為…。

4. I usually ~.

   我通常…。

5. No, I wouldn't ~.

   不，我不會…。

 考題測試 >>>>

 答題示範 2-09.mp3　模擬測驗 2-09-Q.mp3

這個部份共有十題。題目已事先錄音，每題經由耳機播出二次，不印在試卷上。第一至五題，每題回答時間 15 秒；第六至十題，每題回答時間 30 秒。每題播出後，請立即回答。回答時，不一定要用完整句子，但請在作答時間內盡量的表達。（可先聽答題示範音檔，再用模擬測驗音檔進行練習）

1 How long have you been learning English? Do you think it is fun?

你學英語多久了？你覺得有趣嗎？

  參考答案 Let me think about it. Um, I've been learning English since I was an ❶ elementary school student. I don't think it's fun, but I can't choose not to learn it.

讓我想想。呃，我從我小學生的時候學英語到現在。我不覺得有趣，但我不能選擇不要學。

學習解析

❶ elementary school 小學

2 Why do you learn English? When do you think it is useful?

你為什麼學英語？你覺得它什麼時候有用？

 I think having English skills means we can get the latest news around the world. Also, many **publications**❶ are written in English, so I have to learn English to understand them.

我認為擁有英語能力意味著我們可以獲得全世界最新的消息。另外，許多出版物是用英語寫的，所以我必須學英語才能了解它們。

學習解析

❶ publication [ˌpʌblɪˋkeʃən] 出版物 n.

致勝關鍵 KeyPoints

★學英語的好處：

中文	英文
自助旅行	travel by myself
結交外國友人	make foreign friends

PART 2

獲得最新資訊	get the latest information
利用英語出版品	make use of English publications
升遷加薪	get a promotion or raise
通過學校考試	pass exams at school
變得更有自信	become more self-confident
找到更好的工作	find a better job

 ## Do you watch or listen to programs in English? Why or why not?

你會看或聽英語節目嗎？為什麼？

 Yes, I listen to ICRT and watch CNN every day. Even though ❶ I don't always understand what they say, it's still a good way to practice my listening skills.

是的，我每天聽 ICRT、看 CNN。儘管我不是隨時都了解他們說什麼，那還是練習我的聽力的好方法。

學習解析

❶ even though 儘管

 ## Can you share some tips on how to improve English vocabulary? How well do they work for you?

你可以分享一些增進英語單字量的方法嗎？它們對你來說效果如何？

I try to **improve** my English **vocabulary** by reading a lot. When I **encounter** a new word while reading, I can see how it's used, so I think it's better than just **memorizing** single words.
我試圖藉由大量閱讀來增進英語單字量。當我在閱讀時遇到新的單字,我可以看到它是怎麼被使用的,所以我認為這樣比只是記憶個別單字來得好。

學習解析

❶ improve [ɪm`pruv] 改善 v.

❷ vocabulary [və`kæbjə͵lɛrɪ] 詞彙(量) n.

❸ encounter [ɪn`kaʊntɚ] 遭遇 v.

❹ memorize [`mɛmə͵raɪz] 記憶,記住 v.

5 How do you improve your English speaking skills? Do you think you speak English well enough?

你如何改善你的英語口說能力?你認為你的英語說得夠好嗎?

 I make foreign friends and talk with them. Every time I find myself more and more **fluent**, so I think it really works, but I still have a long way to go.
我交外國朋友並且和他們交談。每次我都發現自己越來越流利,所以我想這個方法真的有效,但我還有很長的路要走(有很大的進步空間)。

學習解析

❶ fluent [`fluənt] 流利的 adj.

What may be the reasons that there are many English language schools in Taiwan? Tell me about your opinion.

台灣有許多英語補習班的原因可能是什麼？告訴我你的意見。

 It's simply because English is important. Almost all countries use English to **communicate**❶ with other countries, so in order to be a **global citizen**❷, everyone needs to learn English. A lot of companies **require**❸ their employees to have English skills, and those who don't may have no chance to get a **raise**❹ or **promotion**❺.

就是因為英語很重要的關係。幾乎所有國家都用英語和其他國家溝通，所以為了當個全球公民，每個人都需要學英語。許多公司要求員工具備英語能力，而不具備的人可能會沒有獲得加薪或升職的機會。

學習解析

❶ communicate [kə`mjunə͵ket] 溝通 v.

❷ global citizen 全球公民，世界公民

❸ require [rɪ`kwaɪr] 要求 v.

❹ raise [rez] 加薪 n.

❺ promotion [prə`moʃən] 升職 n.

 Are you a diligent English learner? Tell me about your attitude toward learning English.

你是勤奮的英語學習者嗎？告訴我你對於學習英語的態度。

When it comes to learning English, to be frank❶, I don't work very hard. I know it's important, but I just have no interest❷ in it. Some of my classmates say they love English, but maybe it's because they get good grades in English. Personally, I think geography and history are more interesting, and I do better in these subjects.

說到學英語，坦白說，我並不是很勤奮。我知道它很重要，但我就是對它沒興趣。我有些同學說他們喜愛英語，但或許是因為他們英語成績很好。我個人認為地理和歷史比較有趣，而且我在這兩個科目表現比較好。

學習解析

❶ frank [fræŋk] 坦白的 adj.
❷ interest [`ɪntərɪst] 興趣 n.

8 Do you think children should start learning English before they go to elementary school? Please explain.

你認為孩子應該在上小學前開始學英語嗎？請說明。

 Definitely. Even though some parents fear that learning Chinese and English at the same time may confuse❶ their children, most research❷ suggests❸ that's not the case. A study even suggests that children have to learn a second language before age ten to achieve native-like❹ competence❺. Therefore, I think it's better to learn English earlier.

 當然。儘管有些父母害怕同時學習華語和英語可能會讓他們的小孩困惑，但大部分的研究暗示事實並非如此。一項研究甚至暗示兒童必須在十歲前學第二語言才能達到近似母語人士的能力。所以，我認為早一點學英語比較好。

PART 2

學習解析

❶ confuse [kən`fjuz] 使困惑 v.

❷ research [`rɪsɚtʃ] 研究 n.

❸ suggest [sə`dʒɛst] 暗示 v.

❹ native [`netɪv] 本國人 n.

❺ competence [`kɑmpətəns] 能力 n.

9 What would you consider before you choose a language school? Please explain.

你在選擇語言補習班之前會考慮什麼？請說明。

There would be several things to ❶consider if I were looking for an ❷ideal language school. First, the ❸tuition can't be too high because I'm just a student. Second, I prefer to have a ❹flexible schedule. Last but not least, the ❺location should be near my home so it doesn't take too much time for me to get there.

假如我在找理想的語言補習班的話，有幾件要考慮的事。首先，學費不能太貴，因為我只是個學生。第二，我偏好有彈性的時間安排。最後但同樣重要的是，地點應該離我家近，這樣到那裡才不會花我太多時間。

學習解析

❶ consider [kən`sɪdɚ] 考慮 v.

❷ ideal [aɪ`diəl] 理想的 adj.

❸ tuition [tju`ɪʃən] 學費 n.

❹ flexible [`flɛksəbl] 有彈性的 adj.

❺ location [loˋkeʃən] 地點 n.

致勝關鍵 KeyPoints

★選擇語言補習班時考量的因素：

中文	英文
合理的學費	reasonable tuition
便利的地點	convenient location
專業的教師	professional teachers
好的服務品質	good quality of service
舒適的教室	comfortable classrooms
範圍廣的課程種類	wide range of courses

10 **Why do you want to pass the GEPT test? Tell me the reason you take the test.**

你為什麼想要通過全民英檢考試？告訴我你參加考試的理由。

It's because my company requires its ❶employees to pass the test. It's an ❷international company, which means everyone must be able to communicate in English with people in other countries. Therefore, the company asks us to take the test to prove our English ❸proficiency. If I fail the test, I will not ❹qualify for a raise or promotion.

是因為我的公司要求員工通過考試。那是一家國際公司，意味著每個人都必須能和其他國家的人用英語溝通。所以，公司要我們參加考試來證明英語能力。如果我沒通過考試，我就沒有資格獲得加薪或升職。

學習解析

❶ employee [ˌɛmplɔɪˋi] 受雇員工 n.

❷ international [ˌɪntɚˋnæʃənl̩] 國際的 adj.

❸ proficiency [prəˋfɪʃənsɪ]（例如語言方面的）精通，熟練 n.

❹ qualify for 有得到…的資格

致勝關鍵 KeyPoints

★想通過全民英檢的理由：

中文	英文
建立自信	build self-confidence
公司／學校／父母要求	company's / school's / parents' requirement
有獲得加薪或升職的資格	qualify for a raise or promotion
申請大學	apply to universities
在就業市場中有競爭力	be competitive in the job market
知道考試是什麼樣的	know what the exam is like

最常考生活
主題 *10*

Asking Questions 問問題

主題說明

在 15 秒題目的最後（第 4 或第 5 題），通常會有一個要求對某個對象提出詢問的題目。對方通常是從事某個職業的人，答題時要針對他的職業提出相關的問題，所以平常就要對各種職業的領域有大致的了解。

常見問句句型

1. Your cousin ~ is a ~. Ask him/her some questions about his/her job.
   你的堂／表兄弟姊妹…是…。問他／她一些關於工作的問題。

2. Your neighbor ~ works as a ~. Ask him/her some questions about his/her job.
   你的鄰居…是…。問他／她一些關於工作的問題。

常見回答句型

1. Tell me, do you like to be a ~?
   告訴我，你喜歡當…嗎？

2. Do you make lots of money by ~?
   你藉由…而賺很多錢嗎？

PART 2

3. I want to know more about your job.
   我想要對你的工作有更多了解。

4. Do you get a lot of tips from ~?
   你從…拿到很多小費嗎？

5. Are you busy all the time?
   你總是很忙嗎？

答題示範 2-10.mp3　模擬測驗 2-10-Q.mp3

考題測試 >>>>

這個部份共有五題。題目已事先錄音，每題經由耳機播出二次，不印在試卷上。第一至五題，每題回答時間 15 秒。每題播出後，請立即回答。回答時，不一定要用完整句子，但請在作答時間內盡量的表達。（可先聽答題示範音檔，再用模擬測驗音檔進行練習）

1 **Your neighbor John is a YouTuber. Ask him some questions about his job.**

你的鄰居約翰是一位 YouTuber。向他問一些有關他工作的問題。

參考答案 I heard that you're a famous YouTuber. That's so cool! Tell me, do you enjoy being a Youtuber? Also, I'm curious about your income.

Do you make lots of money by making videos?
我聽說你是一位有名的 YouTuber。那真是太酷了！告訴我，你享受當個 YouTuber 嗎？還有，我很好奇你的收入。你靠著拍影片賺很多錢嗎？

學習解析

❶ YouTuber [`jutjubɚ] 專門在 YouTube 上傳自製影片的人 n.

❷ curious [`kjʊrɪəs] 好奇的 adj.

202

2 Your elementary school classmate George is now an English teacher. Ask him some questions about his job.

你的小學同學喬治現在是一位英語老師。向他問一些有關他工作的問題。

I heard from Jenny, our elementary school classmate, that you're

now an English teacher. Well, I want to know more about your job

and your students. Are they ❷adults or children? Is teaching them

English easy or difficult?

我聽我們的小學同學珍妮說，你現在是英語老師。嗯，我想要知道更多有關
你的工作和學生的事。他們是成人還是小孩？教他們英語簡單還是困難？

學習解析

❶ elementary school 小學

❷ adult [ə`dʌlt] 成年人 n.

3 Your cousin Dan works as a firefighter. Ask him some questions about his job.

你的表哥丹是一位消防員。問他一些有關他工作的問題。

Aunty Helen told me you're a ❶firefighter. I think it's a dangerous job.

I heard that firefighters have a lot of tasks to do besides putting out

fires, such as ❷capturing wild animals like snakes. Is that true?

海倫阿姨告訴我你是消防員。我認為那是危險的工作。聽說消防員除了滅火
以外還有很多工作要做，例如捕捉蛇之類的野生動物。那是真的嗎？

學習解析

❶ firefighter [`faɪrˌfaɪtɚ] 消防員 n.

❷ capture [`kæptʃɚ] 捕捉 v.

 Your ex-coworker Debbie changed jobs. Now she is a singer in a piano bar. Ask her some questions about her new job.

你之前的同事黛比換工作了。現在她是鋼琴酒吧的歌手。問她一些有關她新工作的問題。

I heard that you have a cool new job, a singer! Tell me, what kinds of songs do you sing in the ❶piano bar? English pop songs? Do you get a lot of ❷tips from customers? Do you have a lot of fans?

我聽說你有很酷的新工作,是歌手!告訴我,你在鋼琴酒吧唱什麼樣的歌?英語流行歌嗎?你從顧客那裡得到很多小費嗎?你有很多粉絲嗎?

學習解析

❶ piano bar 鋼琴酒吧

❷ tip [tɪp] 小費 n.

 Your neighbor Kevin is a doctor. Ask him some questions about his job.

你的鄰居凱文是一位醫生。問他一些有關他工作的問題。

參考答案 Hi, I heard you are a doctor. Which hospital do you work in? Are you a ❶surgeon or a ❷physician? How many patients do you have every day? Do you think you have a heavy ❸workload?

嗨，我聽說你是醫生。你在哪間醫院工作？你是外科醫生還是內科醫生？你每天有多少患者？你認為自己的工作量重嗎？

學習解析

❶ surgeon [`sɝdʒən] 外科醫生 n.
❷ physician [fɪ`zɪʃən] 內科醫生 n.
❸ workload [`wɝk͵lod] 工作量 n.

最常考生活
主題 *11*

Giving Advice 建議

主題說明

在 15 秒題目的最後（第 4 或第 5 題），通常會有一個要求對某個對象提出建議的題目。對方可能是在生活上遇到了什麼問題（經常忘東忘西、睡過頭等等），或者要做重要的決定、參加重大的場合等等，答題時必須根據情境做出相關的回答。

常見問句句型

1. Your brother/sister [name] ~. Give him/her some advice.
   你的兄弟／姊妹〔名字〕…。給他／她一些建議。

2. Your friend ~ is going to ~. Give him/her some advice.
   你的朋友…將要…。給他／她一些建議。

常見回答句型

1. Let me give you some advice.
   讓我給你一些建議。

2. Let me give you some suggestions.
   讓我給你一些建議。

3. From my point of view, I think you should ~.

就我來看，我認為你應該…。

4. To be honest, I don't think you should ~.

老實說，我不認為你應該…。

5. I recommend that ~.

我推薦…。

 考 題 測 試 >>>>

答題
示範 2-11.mp3

模擬
測驗 2-11-Q.mp3

這個部份共有五題。題目已事先錄音，每題經由耳機播出二次，不印在試卷上。第一至五題，每題回答時間 15 秒。每題播出後，請立即回答。回答時，不一定要用完整句子，但請在作答時間內盡量的表達。（可先聽答題示範音檔，再用模擬測驗音檔進行練習）

1 Your cousin Peter is going to take the GEPT test. Give him some advice.

你的表弟彼得將要參加全民英檢的考試。給他一些建議。

參考
答案

Hi, bro. Heard that you're going to take the GEPT test. Let me give you some advice. You have to practice speaking, listening, writing and grammar every day. And, of course, you should have a good night's sleep before the test.

嗨，弟。聽說你要參加全民英檢的考試。讓我來給你一些建議。你必須每天練習口說、聽力、寫作與文法。而且當然，你在考試前晚應該睡個好覺。

 學習解析

❶ advice [əd`vaɪs] 忠告，建議 n.

❷ grammar [`græmɚ] 文法 n.

207

PART 2

2 Your friend Tom is going to give a speech. Give him some suggestions.

你的朋友湯姆將要發表演說。給他一些建議。

 I heard you're nervous about giving a speech. First, you should write down what you want to say. And then, you can find some people to be your ❶audience. You'll be more ❷confident if you practice in advance.

我聽說你對於發表演說感到緊張。首先，你應該要寫下你想要說的話。然後，你可以找一些人當你的聽眾。如果你先練習的話，就會比較有信心。

學習解析

❶ audience [`ɔdɪəns] 聽眾 n.

❷ confident [`kɑnfədənt] 有信心的 adj.

3 Your friend Irene is a forgetful person. Give her some suggestions.

你的朋友艾琳是個健忘的人。給她一些建議。

 Irene, you say you're a ❶forgetful person? Let me give you some ❷suggestions. First, you should have enough sleep. People who ❸lack sleep tend to forget things. Second, exercising ❹regularly is also said to improve ❺memory.

艾琳，你說你是個健忘的人嗎？讓我來給你一些建議。首先，你應該要有充足的睡眠。缺乏睡眠的人通常會忘記事情。第二，據說規律運動也會改善記憶力。

學習解析

❶ forgetful [fə`gɛtfəl] 健忘的 adj.

❷ suggestion [sə`dʒɛstʃən] 建議 n.

❸ lack [læk] 缺乏 v.

❹ regularly [`rɛgjələlɪ] 規律地 adv.

❺ memory [`mɛmərɪ] 記憶力 n.

4 Your friend Lily often oversleeps. Give her some suggestions.

你的朋友莉莉常常睡過頭。給她一些建議。

Lily, you overslept again! Let me tell you what you should do. First of all, you should go to bed earlier. Do not stay up late! You should also have at least two alarm clocks to wake you up in the morning.

莉莉，你又睡過頭了！讓我告訴你應該做什麼。首先，你應該早點上床睡覺。不要熬夜！你也應該要有至少兩個鬧鐘在早上叫醒你。

學習解析

❶ oversleep [`ovə`slip] 睡過頭 v.

❷ stay up late 熬夜到很晚

❸ alarm clock 鬧鐘

Your friend Gary received his ex-girlfriend's wedding invitation and is wondering what he should do. Give him some advice.

你的朋友蓋瑞收到他前女友的結婚喜帖（邀請函），並想著應該怎麼做。給他一些建議。

 It may seem ridiculous to you, but I think you should go and give her your best wishes. Now that she is willing to invite you, it means that you're a real friend for her. You don't need to feel embarrassed.

對你來說可能感覺很荒謬，但我認為你應該去給她最深的祝福。既然她願意邀請你，就意味著你對她而言是真正的朋友。你不需要感覺尷尬。

學習解析

❶ willing [ˋwɪlɪŋ] 願意的 adj.

❷ invite [ɪnˋvaɪt] 邀請 v.

❸ embarrassed [ɪmˋbærəst] 感到尷尬的 adj.

最常考生活
主題 *12*

Assumed Situation 假設情況

主題說明

在 30 秒的題目中，通常會有詢問假設狀況的題目，例如「如果你贏了樂透會做什麼」、「如果有機會是否會去火星旅遊」等等。題目往往會使用和現在事實相反的假設語氣過去式，所以回答時也要注意時態的正確性。

常見問句句型

1. If you ~, would you ~?
   如果你…的話，你會…嗎？

2. If you ~, what / which ~ would you ~?
   如果你…的話，你會…什麼…？

常見回答句型

1. If I were ~, I would ~.
   假如我是…，我會…。

2. If I had ~, I would ~.
   假如我有…，我會…。

3. I would definitely ~ if I were~.
   假如我是…，我一定會…

PART 2

4. I think I would ~.
   我想我會…。

5. I'm not sure if I would ~.
   我不確定我會不會…。

考題測試 >>>>

答題示範
2-12.mp3

模擬測驗
2-12-Q.mp3

這個部份共有五題。題目已事先錄音，每題經由耳機播出二次，不印在試卷上。第一至五題，每題回答時間 30 秒。每題播出後，請立即回答。回答時，不一定要用完整句子，但請在作答時間內盡量的表達。（可先聽答題示範音檔，再用模擬測驗音檔進行練習）

1 If you won the lottery, what would you do?

假如你中樂透，你會做什麼？

參考答案

I would **definitely** travel around the world. I like traveling, and I learn a lot of things every time I go on a trip. Northern Europe would be the first place I visit because I've heard that **auroras** are **extremely** beautiful there. I really want to see the **sight** myself.

我絕對會環遊世界。我喜歡旅遊，而且每次旅遊我都學到很多事情。北歐會是我第一個拜訪的地方，因為我聽說那裡極光非常美。我真的很想親自看到那個景象。

學習解析

❶ definitely [`dɛfənɪtlɪ] 絕對 adv.

❷ aurora [ɔ`rorə] 極光 n.

❸ extremely [ɪk`strimlɪ] 極度地 adv.

212

❹ sight [saɪt] 景象 n.

 If you could buy a big mansion, where in Taiwan would you prefer it to be located?

假如你能買一棟大別墅，你會偏好它位於台灣的哪裡？

> **參考答案**
>
> I would certainly choose Taipei City or New Taipei City. Needless to say, it's more convenient to live there than in any other area. In the Greater Taipei Area, there are good ❶medical institutions and modern ❷traffic facilities. What's more, there are also many beautiful parks, ❸delectable restaurants and famous ❹attractions to visit.
>
> 我一定會選擇台北市或新北市。不用說，住在那裡比在其他任何地區來得便利。在大台北地區，有好的醫療機構和現代的交通設施。而且，還有許多美麗的公園、美味的餐廳和有名的景點可以拜訪。

學習解析

❶ medical institution 醫療機構

❷ traffic facility 交通設施

❸ delectable [dɪ`lɛktəbl] 令人愉快的，美味的 adj.

❹ attraction [ə`trækʃən] 景點 n.

 If today were the last day of your life, how would you like to spend it?

假如今天是你生命中最後一天，你會想要怎麼度過？

I would go back to my ❶hometown to visit my parents and tell them how much I love them. I would also visit some childhood friends and talk with them about those good old days. If possible, I would also like to say "thank you" to all the people who have helped me and ❷apologize to those who I've hurt.

我會回到我的家鄉看我的父母,並且告訴他們我有多愛他們。我也會拜訪一些兒時朋友,跟他們聊聊過去的美好時光。如果可能的話,我也想要對所有幫助過我的人說謝謝,並且對我傷害過的人道歉。

學習解析

❶ hometown [`hom`taʊn] 故鄉 n.

❷ apologize [ə`pɑlə,dʒaɪz] 道歉 v.

4 If you had the ability to see someone's future, would you tell them what will happen to them?

假如你有看見某人未來的能力,你會告訴他們將發生在他們身上的事嗎?

 That depends. If I saw something good, I wouldn't say a word because that's not my business. On the other hand, if I saw something bad, I would try to give the person some ❶hints to help ❷avoid the bad luck. However, to be frank, it seems to me that having this kind of ability isn't a good thing.

那要看情況。如果我看到好事,我什麼也不會說,因為那不關我的事。另一方面,如果我看到壞事,我會試著給那個人一些暗示來幫忙避開壞運。不過,老實說,擁有這種能力在我看來不是件好事。

學習解析

❶ hint [hɪnt] 暗示 n.

❷ avoid [ə`vɔɪd] 避開 v.

 If you were the President, what would you do to make our country better?
假如你是總統，你會做什麼讓我們的國家更好？

 This is a serious question. First, I would create more job¹ opportunities and lower the unemployment rate². Second, I would definitely promote³ equality⁴. Everyone should have equal rights to express their points of view⁵. Third, I would care more about environmental pollution⁶, especially air pollution in the middle of Taiwan.

這是一個嚴肅的問題。首先，我會創造更多的就業機會，並且降低失業率。第二，我一定會促進平權。每個人都應該有平等的權利來表達自己的觀點。第三，我會更關心環境污染，尤其是台灣中部的空氣污染。

學習解析

❶ job opportunity 工作機會

❷ unemployment rate 失業率

❸ promote [prə`mot] 促進 v.

❹ equality [i`kwɑlətɪ] 平等 n.

❺ environmental pollution 環境污染

最常考生活
主題 *13*

Advantages or Disadvantages
好處或壞處

主題說明

在 30 秒的題目中，通常會有詢問做某事的好處或壞處的題目，例如「租房子而不買房子有什麼好處或壞處」、「搭大眾運輸工具上班有什麼好處或壞處」。回答時可以兩方面都討論，或者只討論其中一方面。

常見問句句型

1. What are some advantages or disadvantages of [-ing] ~?
   …的一些好處或壞處是什麼？

常見回答句型

1. In my opinion, there are a lot of advantages of ~.
   就我來看，…有很多好處。

2. From my point of view, there are some benefits of ~.
   就我來看，…有一些好處。

3. Apparently, ~ brings many benefits.

　明顯地，…會帶來許多好處。

4. For me, there are some disadvantages of ~.

　對我而言，…有一些壞處。

5. Whether ~ is good or bad depends on how you see it.

　…是好或壞取決於你如何看待它。

考 題 測 試 >>>>

答題示範 🎧 2-13.mp3　　模擬測驗 🎧 2-13-Q.mp3

這個部份共有五題。題目已事先錄音，每題經由耳機播出二次，不印在試卷上。第一至五題，每題回答時間 30 秒。每題播出後，請立即回答。回答時，不一定要用完整句子，但請在作答時間內盡量的表達。（可先聽答題示範音檔，再用模擬測驗音檔進行練習）

1　What are some advantages or disadvantages of working from home?

在家工作的一些好處或壞處是什麼？

參考答案

For some jobs, working from home is better than going to the office. Working from home can save you commuting time, and you can still handle your work and communicate with your colleagues on the Internet. However, you may be less productive at home because there are many distractions, such as family members, chores, and noises.

對於一些工作來說，在家工作比去辦公室來得好。在家工作可以為你省下通勤時間，而你還是可以在網路上處理工作並且和同事溝通。不過，你在家裡可能生產力會比較低，因為有很多讓人分心的事，例如家人、家事和噪音。

學習解析

❶ commuting time 通勤時間

❷ handle [`hændl] 處理 v.

❸ colleague [`kɑlig] 同事 n.

❹ productive [prə`dʌktɪv] 有生產力的 adj.

❺ distraction [dɪ`strækʃən] 令人分心的事物 n.

What are some advantages or disadvantages of working out at a gym?

在健身房健身的一些好處或壞處是什麼？

The gym is a great place to do ❶weight training because there are all kinds of equipment there. What's more, the ❷professional ❸trainers there can teach you how to do exercise without getting hurt. For those who are not interested in ❹building muscle, there are also ❺aerobic classes to take. After working out, you can take a shower and relax in the ❻sauna or ❼steam room there.

健身房是做重量訓練的好地方，因為那裡有各種設備。而且，那裡的專業教練可以教你如何運動而不受傷。對於增長肌肉沒興趣的人，也有有氧課程可以上。運動之後，你可以在那裡淋浴，並且在三溫暖烤箱或蒸氣室放鬆。

學習解析

❶ weight training 重量訓練

❷ professional [prə`fɛʃənl] 職業的，專業的 adj.

❸ trainer [`trenɚ]（例如健身房的）教練 n.

❹ build muscle 使肌肉增長

❺ aerobic class 有氧課程

❻ sauna [`saʊnə] 三溫暖烤箱 n.

❼ steam room 蒸氣室

What are some advantages or disadvantages of renting a residence instead of buying one?

租房而不買房的一些好處或壞處是什麼？

One advantage is that I don't have to prepare a lot of money. It takes millions of (Taiwan) dollars to buy an apartment, and I can't afford ❶ buying one. However, the renting experience is not always pleasant, ❷ especially when the landlord does not take the responsibility to make ❸ ❹ repairs. It'll also be a nightmare if the landlord raises the rent too ❺ much.

一項好處是我不必準備很多錢。買公寓要花（台幣）好幾百萬元，我買不起。然而，租賃經驗並不總是愉快的，尤其是房東不負起修理東西的責任時。如果房東漲太多房租，也會是個惡夢。

學習解析

❶ afford [ə`ford] 負擔得起…

❷ pleasant [`plɛzənt] 令人愉快的 adj.

❸ landlord [`lænd͵lord] 房東 n.

❹ responsibility [rɪ͵spɑnsə`bɪlətɪ] 責任 n.

❺ nightmare [`naɪt͵mɛr] 惡夢 n.

4 What are some advantages or disadvantages of taking public transportation to work?

搭乘大眾運輸工具上班的一些好處或壞處是什麼？

 I go to work by bus every day, and I think there are lots of benefits ❶ of doing so. I don't need to worry about parking ❷, and I can save the money of maintaining ❸ a car or motorcycle. Besides, taking public transportation ❹ is friendlier to the environment ❺. Some say they don't want to waste their time waiting for a bus, but with bus tracking ❻ apps, that's not a problem anymore.

我每天搭公車上班，我認為這麼做有很多好處。我不需要擔心停車的問題，也可以省下保養汽車或機車的錢。而且，搭乘大眾運輸工具比較環保。有些人說他們不想浪費時間等公車，但有了公車追蹤 app，那就不再是個問題了。

學習解析

❶ benefit [`bɛnəfɪt] 利益，好處 n.

❷ parking [`pɑrkɪŋ] 停車，停車處 n.

❸ maintain [men`ten] 維護，保養 v.

❹ public transportation 大眾交通運輸

❺ friendly to the environment 對環境友善→環保

❻ track [træk] 追蹤 v.

5 What are some advantages or disadvantages of ordering food delivery?

叫食物外送的一些好處或壞處是什麼？

 Apparently, ordering food delivery❶ is convenient for people who don't have time or just don't want to go out. With just a little extra money, you can have your favorite food delivered to your door and enjoy it ❷in the comfort of your home. But be careful! You may get too lazy to even step out of your home!

明顯地，叫食物外送對於沒有時間或者只是不想出門的人而言很便利。只要一點額外的錢，就可以讓人把你最愛的食物送到門口，並且在家舒服地享用。但要小心！你可能變得太懶而根本不出門！

學習解析

❶ delivery [dɪˋlɪvərɪ] 配送 n.
❷ in the comfort of one's home 在家舒服地…

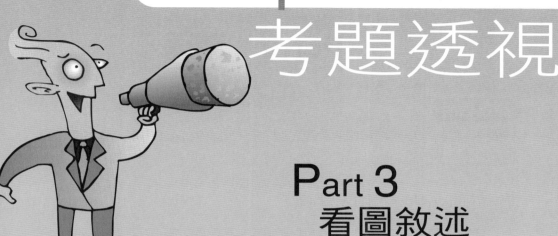

Chapter 2
考題透視

Part 3
看圖敘述

高分技巧

1. 先看圖，迅速判斷圖片的主題。

2. 迅速瀏覽題目，並對照照片找出會使用到的字彙。

3. 若你不知道圖中事物的英文單字，試著用關係代名詞及其他簡單的單字去解釋。

4. 如果回答完題目所提示的問題後還有時間，請儘量針對圖片其他部分做敘述，甚至可以談論這張照片帶給你的感受及啟示。

5. 永遠記住一句最重要的口說應試守則：「老實無用，牽拖至上」。

最常考主
題圖片 1

Ferry　渡輪

題目說明

下面有一張圖片及四個相關的問題,請在一分半鐘內完成作答。作答時,請
直接回答,不需將題號及題目唸出。

首先請利用 30 秒的時間看圖及問題。

1. 這可能是什麼地方?你怎麼知道?
2. 圖片中的人在做什麼?
3. 你曾經做過類似的活動嗎?告訴我你的經驗。
4. 如果還有時間,請描述圖片中人物的穿著和景物。

參考答案

3-01.mp3

I see a ferry❶ docked❷ at the pier❸. Some people are walking towards the ferry, so I think, of course they're going to board the ferry and go ahead to their destination❹. We call these people passengers❺. The weather seems nice, so it can't be a bumpy❻ ride. Therefore, these passengers won't have seasickness❼, I guess. Have I ever taken a ferry? Yes, I've taken a ferry before. I remember when I was in college in the south of Taiwan, I often took a ferry to a famous beach. It took only fifteen minutes to cross the water to the other side. And I also remember the price of the ticket was about fifty dollars. I think the ferry in the picture is much bigger than what I took at that time.

中文理解

我看見一艘渡輪停泊在碼頭。有些人正在走向這艘渡輪，所以我認為他們當然是要登上渡輪，並且前往他們的目的地。我們把這些人叫做乘客。天氣似乎不錯，所以不大可能會是一趟顛簸的航程。因此，我猜這些乘客將不會暈船。我曾經搭過渡輪嗎？是的，我以前搭過渡輪。我記得當我在台灣南部讀大學時，我經常搭渡輪到一座有名的海灘。只要花十五分鐘的時間便可渡過水域到另一邊。我也記得渡輪的票價大約五十元。我想這張照片裡的渡輪比我當時搭的要大得多。

學習解析

❶ ferry [`fɛrɪ] 渡輪 n.

❷ dock [dɑk] 使停靠碼頭 v.

❸ pier [pɪr] 碼頭 n.

❹ destination [ˌdɛstə`neʃən] 目的地 n.

❺ passenger [`pæsəndʒɚ] 乘客 n.

❻ bumpy [`bʌmpɪ] 顛簸的 adj.

❼ seasickness [`siˌsɪknɪs] 暈船 n.

必殺萬用句

I see...

我看到…

　　有很多平常能言善道的人，一到了考試的時候就突然不知道要講些什麼。其實最主要的原因，並不是他不知道要講什麼，而是他雖然有很多東西可以講，卻一時找不到起頭。英文也是一樣，有許多簡單的句子、簡單的單字等著你行雲流水地運用，千萬不要因為顧慮太多而造成「卡彈」的現象。像這種時候，I see... 就是很容易引導說話內容的開頭，反正題目一定是要你敘述這張照片不是嗎？想要特別說明是照片的哪個部分，可以在前面加上 on the left/right/top/bottom of the picture（在照片的左邊／右邊／上面／下面）。

最常考主
題圖片 2

Aquarium　水族館

題目說明

下面有一張圖片及四個相關的問題，請在一分半鐘內完成作答。作答時，請
直接回答，不需將題號及題目唸出。

首先請利用 30 秒的時間看圖及問題。

1. 這可能是什麼地方？
2. 圖片中的人在做什麼？
3. 你曾經參觀過類似的活動嗎？當時你有什麼感覺？
4. 如果還有時間，請描述圖片中人物的穿著和景物。

PART 3

參考答案

In the picture, there are some spectators① watching a dolphin show. Such shows can be seen in some aquariums②. The spectators are fascinated③ by the show, I guess. In the picture, I can see a pool and two dolphins jumping over the water. Wow! ***What an amazing performance!*** There is also a trainer④ standing in the corner. I think he's giving some instructions⑤ to the dolphins. I have watched a dolphin show before. It was impressive. It was when I was a child. My parents took me to the Ocean Park in Hong Kong, and we saw the spectacular⑥ show. I was amazed that dolphins can do so many tricks. As a child, I enjoyed the show a lot, but now I wonder whether dolphins in aquariums are happy or not.

中文理解

在照片中，有一些在看海豚表演的觀眾。這種表演可以在一些水族館看到。我猜這些觀眾對表演很入迷。在照片中，我可以看到一個池子，和兩隻正在跳過水面的海豚。哇！真是令人驚喜的表演！還有一位訓練員站在角落。我想他正在給予這些海豚一些指示。我以前看過海豚秀。那很令人印象深刻。那是在我小的時候。我的父母帶我到香港的海洋公園，我們看了那場很棒的表演。我很驚訝海豚能玩這麼多把戲。身為小孩，我很喜歡那場表演，但現在我想知道水族館裡的海豚是否快樂。

學習解析

❶ spectator [spɛk`tetɚ] 觀眾 n.

❷ aquarium [ə`kwɛrɪəm] 水族箱，水族館 n.

❸ fascinated [`fæsn̩ˌetɪd] 入迷的 adj.

❹ trainer [`trenɚ] 訓練員 n.

❺ instruction [ɪn`strʌkʃən] 指示 n.

❻ spectacular [spɛk`tækjəlɚ] 壯觀的，驚人的 adj.

必殺萬用句

What an amazing performance!

真是令人驚喜的表演！

　　除了敘述照片裡的東西，也可以把你自己對照片的感覺加進來。這個時候，像這樣的感嘆句就非常有用了。例如風景的照片，通常可以用 What a beautiful sight!（真是美麗的景象啊！）來評論。也許評分老師並不認為這張照片漂亮，但漂亮與否是個人觀點，就算評分老師的意見和你不同，也不會因此扣你的分數。當然，有時候說景色很美還是有點牽強，例如照片是一家便利商店，或者警察在開罰單，硬要說很美就有點離譜了，但我們還是可以用另一個句型相似，但適用範圍更廣的句子：What an interesting picture!（真是有趣的照片！）。我就是覺得警察開罰單的照片有趣，不行嗎？

最常考主
題圖片 *3*

Park 公園

題目說明

下面有一張圖片及四個相關的問題,請在一分半鐘內完成作答。作答時,請
直接回答,不需將題號及題目唸出。

首先請利用 30 秒的時間看圖及問題。

1. 這可能是什麼地方?
2. 圖片中的人在做什麼?
3. 你通常會去這個地方做什麼事?
4. 如果還有時間,請描述圖片中人物的穿著和景物。

3-03.mp3

參考答案

This is a small park, just like other parks in my **neighborhood**[1]. Some people in the picture are walking in the park. I see a man with his kid playing. The kid is swinging on a swing. In the picture, I can see some buildings and some trees. *It looks like* it's a quiet afternoon because there are not many people in this **community**[2] park. Sometimes, I take my children to a community park like this one and let them play there. I have one boy and two girls. They're five, six, and seven years old. There is a seesaw, a swing, and a jogging track in the park near my house. I strongly believe we should have more parks in our city. It's not only a place for us to relax and do some exercise, but also a place for kids to run and play.

中文理解　　　　這是一座小公園，就像是我居住區域的其他公園一樣。照片裡的一些人正在公園裡走路。我看到一名男子帶著在玩耍的小孩。小孩正在盪鞦韆。在這張照片中，我可以看見一些大樓以及一些樹木。看起來這是一個安靜的下午，因為沒有很多人在這社區公園裡。有時候，我會帶我的小孩去像這樣的社區公園，並且讓他們在那裡玩。我有一個兒子和兩個女兒。他們是五歲、六歲與七歲。在我家附近的公園裡有蹺蹺板、鞦韆與慢跑道。我強烈地認為我們的城市裡應該要有更多公園。公園不但是一個讓我們放鬆和運動的地方，也是讓小孩奔跑並玩耍的地方。

231

學習解析

❶ neighborhood [`nebɚˌhʊd] 鄰近地區，街坊 n.
❷ community [kə`mjunətɪ] 社區 n.

必殺萬用句

It looks like...

看起來...

　　要對照片中的情況進行推測的時候，就可以用 It looks like... 表達「看起來（好像）…）」的意思，請注意這個用法的後面是接子句，可以把推測的內容完整表達出來。當然，也有用「名詞 looks like 名詞」表示「某個人事物看起來像什麼」的用法，在表達地點的時候特別好用。照片題幾乎一定會問你這是什麼地方，這時候就可以說 This place looks like...（這個地方看起來像…），然後再補充說你在照片中看到什麼，證明你的推測。

最常考主
題圖片 *4*

Pet　寵物

題目說明

下面有一張圖片及四個相關的問題,請在一分半鐘內完成作答。作答時,請直接回答,不需將題號及題目唸出。

首先請利用 30 秒的時間看圖及問題。

1. 這可能是什麼地方?你怎麼知道?
2. 圖片中的人在做什麼?
3. 你曾經做過類似的活動嗎?你喜歡嗎?為什麼?
4. 如果還有時間,請描述圖片中人物的穿著和景物。

3-04.mp3

參考答案

I see a woman and a dog in the picture. The woman is holding a ball and trying to get the dog's **attention**. Maybe she is training her pet or just playing with it. I also see a computer in the picture, so *I guess* they're not at home. Maybe they're in an office. The dog in the picture is so cute. I also have a pet dog. He's a little **beagle**. Very often, we play together, and we play throw-and-catch, too. I think keeping a pet is a good idea because pets can be your friends, and they can keep you in a good mood by simply staying by your side. But I'm wondering why the woman can play with her dog at this time. Shouldn't she work hard at the office? Or maybe it's her break time? Anyway, the picture is really interesting.

中文理解

我看到照片裡有一名女子和一隻狗。這名女子握著一顆球，並且試圖引起這隻狗的注意。也許她正在訓練她的寵物，或者只是在跟牠玩。我也看見照片裡有一台電腦，所以我猜他們不是在家中。也許他們是在辦公室裡。照片裡的狗很可愛。我也有一隻寵物狗。他是一隻小小的米格魯。我們很常在一起玩，我們也玩丟球與接球的遊戲。我認為養一隻寵物是好主意，因為寵物可以當你的朋友，也可以只是待在你身邊就讓你保持好心情。但我疑惑女子為什麼可以在這個時間和狗玩。她在辦公室不是應該認真工作嗎？或者也許現在是她的休息時間？不管怎樣，這張照片實在很有趣。

學習解析

❶ attention [əˋtɛnʃən] 注意 n.
❷ beagle [ˋbigl̩] 小獵犬（米格魯） n.

必殺萬用句

I guess...

我猜…

　　讓我們仔細想一下，當我們在課堂上，或者在模擬測驗練習口說的時候，有什麼表達方式是用得很氾濫的？I think... 應該是排行榜上的前幾名吧。在教學的時候，我經常聽到許多學生習慣性說出 I think...，其實這也沒有什麼錯，但如果過度使用，就會讓人覺得你的講話方式過於格式化而呆板，所以偶爾改用推測的說法 I guess... 或者副詞 probably（可能），會讓你的談話內容更加多樣化。

最常考主
題圖片 5

Lake 湖

題目說明

下面有一張圖片及四個相關的問題,請在一分半鐘內完成作答。作答時,請直接回答,不需將題號及題目唸出。

首先請利用 30 秒的時間看圖及問題。

1. 這可能是什麼地方?
2. 圖片中的人在做什麼?
3. 你曾經做過類似的活動嗎?你喜歡嗎?為什麼?
4. 如果還有時間,請描述圖片中人物的穿著和景物。

參考答案

The people in the picture are fishing in the lake. I see three people in total in the picture. They're all fishing. One of them is under a big umbrella. The weather must be hot, I guess. There is also a big bird in the picture. Is it waiting for fish, too? It's an interesting picture. *Everything in the picture seems* so quiet. I like to go to the lake. However, I don't know how to fish. I go there to watch other people fishing, or just ❶roam near the lake. You know what? I always feel ❷light-hearted after taking a walk by the lake. As I see it, ❸modern people are ❹stressed out every day, so we all should find some ways to ❺release our ❻pressure. Do you agree?

中文理解

照片裡的人們正在釣湖裡的魚。我看見照片裡總共有三個人。他們都在釣魚。其中有一個人在大型的雨傘下面。我猜天氣一定很熱。照片中還有一隻大鳥。牠也在等魚嗎？真是有趣的圖片。照片中的一切看起來都很安靜。我喜歡去湖邊。然而，我不知道怎麼釣魚。我去那裡是看其他人釣魚，或者只是在湖附近漫步。你知道嗎？在湖邊散步後，我總是覺得很愉快。在我看來，現代人每天壓力都很大，所以我們都應該找一些方法來釋放壓力。你同意嗎？

學習解析

❶ roam [rom] 漫步 v.

❷ light-hearted [`laɪt`hɑrtɪd] 輕鬆愉快的 adj.

❸ modern [`mɑdərn] 現代的 adj.

❹ stressed out 感到有壓力的

❺ release [rɪ`lis] 釋放 v.

❻ pressure [`prɛʃər] 壓力 n.

必殺萬用句

Everything in the picture seems...

照片中的一切看起來都…

　　通常照片裡都有一個「焦點」，但也常有出現很多事物的情況，不管是一群動物或一堆東西，只要在 Everything in the picture seems... 後面接上形容詞，就可以表達你對這一群事物的感覺。如果是一群人，則可以說 everyone，或者用 They all look very...，對於人、事、物都可以使用。另外還有一個口試的小技巧，就是多多使用主詞 they，因為 they 沒有 he/she 的性別區分，也不會產生「第三人稱單數」的動詞變化，比較不容易因為這些小細節而失分，所以能用 they 的話就儘量使用吧。

最常考主
題圖片 6

Restaurant 餐廳

下面有一張圖片及四個相關的問題,請在一分半鐘內完成作答。作答時,請
直接回答,不需將題號及題目唸出。

首先請利用 30 秒的時間看圖及問題。

1. 這可能是什麼地方?你怎麼知道?
2. 圖片中的人在做什麼?
3. 你曾經去過類似的地方嗎?你喜歡那裡的什麼?告訴我你
   的經驗。
4. 如果還有時間,請描述圖片中人物的穿著和景物。

3-06.mp3

參考答案

　　The people in the picture are having lunch or dinner in a Cantonese restaurant. More specifically, *I think this picture was taken* in a dim sum house. It's a place where you can drink tea as well as having some dim sum. I bet it's a popular restaurant, for there are so many customers in it. There's also a server in the picture. It looks like she's busy serving food. Cantonese cuisine is renowned for its steamed food. Have you ever tried "Barbecue Pork Buns" or "Turnip Cakes"? They're both my favorites. I've been to this kind of restaurant many times, and I always recommend my foreign friends to try Cantonese food at least once or twice.

中文理解

　　這張圖片裡的人正在廣式餐廳吃午餐或是晚餐。更具體地說，我認為這張照片是在港式點心餐廳（茶樓）拍的。那是你可以喝茶並且吃一些港式點心的地方。我敢打賭這是一間受歡迎的餐廳，因為裡面有很多顧客。照片裡也有一位服務員。看起來她忙著上菜。廣式烹飪以蒸的食物聞名。你曾經試過「叉燒包」或「蘿蔔糕」嗎？它們都是我的最愛。我去過這種餐廳很多次，我也總是推薦我的外國友人至少嘗試廣式料理一兩次。

學習解析

❶ Cantonese [ˌkæntəˋniz] 廣東的 adj.

❷ dim sum [dɪmˋsʌm] 廣式點心 n.

❸ server [ˋsɝvɚ] （餐廳負責上菜的）服務員 n.

❹ cuisine [kwɪˋzin] 烹飪，烹調法 n.

❺ renowned [rɪˋnaʊnd] 著名的 adj.

❻ Barbecue Pork Bun 叉燒包

❼ Turnip Cake 蘿蔔糕（turnip 是蕪菁，而白蘿蔔正確的說法是 radish，但習慣上稱為 turnip cake 的情況還是比較多）

❽ recommend [ˌrɛkəˋmɛnd] 推薦 v.

必殺萬用句

I think this picture was taken...

我認為這張照片是在…拍的

　　猜測照片拍攝的地點是很好的破題方式。看圖敘述的第一個問題往往是「這是什麼地方」，很多人會直接說 This is a park.（這是公園）、This is a school.（這是學校），但如果改成比較迂迴的說法，除了可以增加回答的長度，也可以讓你的答案顯得和別人不一樣。雖然同樣是表達地點，但 I think this picture was taken... 可以展現出你除了直述句以外，也會使用被動語態。

最常考主
題圖片 7

Pool 水池

題目說明

下面有一張圖片及四個相關的問題,請在一分半鐘內完成作答。作答時,請
直接回答,不需將題號及題目唸出。

首先請利用 30 秒的時間看圖及問題。

1. 這可能是什麼地方?你怎麼知道?
2. 圖片中的人在做什麼?
3. 你曾經做過類似的活動嗎?告訴我你的經驗。
4. 如果還有時間,請描述圖片中人物的穿著和景物。

參考答案

3-07.mp3

In the picture, there are many people playing in the pool. I guess the weather is hot, so they need to cool themselves down in the water. I also see two people sitting by the pool. They aren't playing in the water. They're ❶sunbathing. I see a warning sign hanging on the metal ❷railing. It says "0.25 meters", and there are two "no ❸diving" symbols. That is to say, you can't dive into the pool because the ❹shallow end is only 25 centimeters deep. In summer, I'll definitely go to a swimming pool. When it's ❺extremely hot, I go swimming four times a week. By the way, I think it's also nice to go to the beach. I remember going surfing and ❻water skiing with my classmates in Kenting. Even though there are some risks, we can safely enjoy water sports as long as we follow safety ❼guidelines.

中文理解

在這張照片裡，有很多人正在水池裡玩。我猜天氣很熱，所以他們需要在水裡讓自己降溫。我也看見兩個人坐在水池旁。他們沒有在水裡玩。他們在做日光浴。我看見一個警告標誌掛在金屬的欄杆上。上面寫著「0.25 公尺」，還有兩個「禁止跳水」的符號。也就是說，你不能跳進水池，因為淺的那邊只有 25 公分深。在夏天，我一定會去游泳池。天氣非常熱的時候，我一個禮拜游泳四次。對了，我認為去海灘也很好。我記得和同學去墾丁衝浪、滑水。儘管有一些危險性，但只要我們遵守安全守則，就可以安全地享受水上運動。

PART 3

學習解析

❶ sunbathe [ˋsʌnˌbeð] 做日光浴 v.

❷ railing [ˋrelɪŋ] 欄杆 n.

❸ dive [daɪv] 跳水 v.

❹ shallow [ˋʃælo] 淺的 adj.

❺ extremely [ɪkˋstrimlɪ] 極度地 adv.

❻ water skiing 滑水（讓船隻牽引而在水面上滑行）

❼ guideline [ˋgaɪdˌlaɪn] 指導方針 n.

必殺萬用句

In the picture, there is/are...

這張照片裡有⋯

　　從小到大，很多人會被灌輸一個觀念：「破題句要特別、特殊，要能語驚四座」，尤其在國文作文的時候，第一句絕對不能隨便寫寫。如果題目是「家人」，第一句寫「我家有四個人」，這樣的作文絕對拿不到高分。但英語口說測驗就不是這麼回事了，想要刻意構思「令人印象深刻的第一句」，反而會讓你遲遲不敢開口。想要表達照片裡有什麼，就老老實實地說 In the picture, there is/are...，又有何不可呢？

最常考主
題圖片 *8*

Meeting　會議

題目說明

下面有一張圖片及四個相關的問題，請在一分半鐘內完成作答。作答時，請
直接回答，不需將題號及題目唸出。

首先請利用 30 秒的時間看圖及問題。

1. 這可能是什麼地方？你怎麼知道？
2. 圖片中的人在做什麼？
3. 你曾經做過類似的活動嗎？當時你有什麼感覺？告訴我你
   的經驗。
4. 如果還有時間，請描述圖片中人物的穿著和景物。

PART 3

3-08.mp3

The people in the picture are in a meeting room. *Obviously*, they're having a meeting and discussing some issues. There are eight people in total. The man standing in the front is talking about something or setting the record straight. Maybe he is a team leader who's had a change of heart and is explaining what he wants to change. As for me, yes, I've attended lots of meetings, but honestly, I'm not a gifted leader, despite the fact that I'm a supervisor. I'm not good at speaking. When I have to lead a meeting, I always ask my deputy to do it for me. In return, I would buy him lunch. I'm so ashamed to talk about this, but I also believe it's OK not to be eloquent. Sometimes talk is cheap, and hard work is what will really pay off.

中文理解

這張照片裡的人在會議室裡。很明顯地,他們正在開會,並且在討論一些事宜。總共有八個人。站在前面的男子正在談論什麼,或者是在澄清事實。或許他是改變了想法的團隊領導者,正在說明他想要改變什麼。至於我,是的,我參加過許多會議,但老實說,我不是天生的領導者,儘管事實上我是主管。我不擅長說話。當我必須主持會議時,我總是請我的副手代替我做。為了回報他,我會請他吃午餐。我對於談論這件事感到羞愧,但我也相信口才不好沒關係。有時候光說是沒用的,努力才會真的有所回報。

學習解析

❶ set the record straight 澄清事實

❷ supervisor [`supɚˋvaɪzɚ] 監督者，主管 n.

❸ deputy [`dɛpjətɪ] 副手 n.

❹ ashamed [əˋʃemd] 感到羞愧的 adj.

❺ eloquent [`ɛləkwənt] 雄辯的，口才好的 adj.

必殺萬用句

Obviously...

顯然…

　　對於照片中不確定的細節，可以表達自己不太清楚那是什麼，但如果照片很明確地顯示某種情況或某些事物，就不適合用籠統的方式回答。尤其是照片的地點或場合，我們往往可以直接看出來，這時候直接用 Obviously... 來表達，不但可以讓人感受到你的自信，也可以脫離 I think... 這種老套的開頭方式。當然，在這之後還是可以用「我不太清楚…」的方式來拖延時間，例如本題就可以說 Obviously, they're having a meeting, but I'm not sure what they're talking about.。畢竟，如果只看照片就知道他們在說什麼，那也太厲害了吧！

最常考主
題圖片 9

Airport　機場

題目說明

下面有一張圖片及四個相關的問題,請在一分半鐘內完成作答。作答時,請直接回答,不需將題號及題目唸出。

首先請利用 30 秒的時間看圖及問題。

1. 這可能是什麼地方?你怎麼知道?
2. 圖片中的人在做什麼?
3. 你曾經去過類似的地方嗎?告訴我你的經驗。
4. 如果還有時間,請描述圖片中人物的穿著和景物。

參考答案

3-09.mp3

The people in the picture are in an airport. The aircraft is on the parking apron. There is a shuttle bus in the picture, too. Some people, or passengers, are walking to the shuttle bus with their baggage. Maybe they're going to the terminal. The car in the picture looks like a police car. Maybe the police want to investigate something. *When people* go abroad, *they need to go to* an airport. I've been to many airports in different countries. Many of them are equipped with state-of-the-art equipment. In contrast, I think the airports in Taiwan need a lot of improvement. I believe those who have been to Singapore or Tokyo would agree with me.

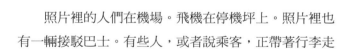

中文理解

　　照片裡的人們在機場。飛機在停機坪上。照片裡也有一輛接駁巴士。有些人，或者說乘客，正帶著行李走向接駁巴士。也許他們正要去航站大廈。在圖片裡的車看起來像是一輛警車。也許警方想要偵查某件事。當人們要出國時，他們需要去機場。我去過不同國家的許多機場。其中許多機場配備最先進的設備。相對地，我認為台灣的機場需要許多改善。我相信去過新加坡或東京的人會同意我所說的。

學習解析

❶ parking apron 停機坪

❷ shuttle bus 接駁巴士

❸ baggage [`bægɪdʒ] 行李 n.

❹ terminal [`tɝmənl] 航廈 n.

❺ investigate [ɪn`vɛstə‚get] 調查 v.

❻ equip [ɪ`kwɪp] 使配備 v.

❼ state-of-the-art 最先進的

❽ equipment [ɪ`kwɪpmənt] 設備 n.

❾ improvement [ɪm`pruvmənt] 改善 n.

必殺萬用句

When people..., they need to go to...
當人們…時，他們需要去…

　　看圖敘述的考題往往是某個具體場所的照片，例如這一題是機場，其他考題也許會是銀行、博物館等等。像這種有明確功能的場所，使用 When people..., they need to go to... 這個句型，就可以很簡單地說明場所的功能，並且表示你對圖片內容有正確的理解。

最常考主題
圖片 10

Hotel　旅館

題目說明

下面有一張圖片及四個相關的問題，請在一分半鐘內完成作答。作答時，請直接回答，不需將題號及題目唸出。

首先請利用 30 秒的時間看圖及問題。

1. 這可能是什麼地方？你怎麼知道？
2. 圖片中的人在做什麼？
3. 你曾經去過類似的地方嗎？告訴我你的經驗。
4. 如果還有時間，請描述圖片中人物的穿著和景物。

3-10.mp3

The people in the picture are in a hotel. One customer is standing with a **①suitcase** at the **②counter**. *Maybe* she's checking in, *or maybe* she's checking out. The person behind the counter is the **③receptionist**, and she's serving the customer. Maybe she's saying, "Miss, here is your room key. You're in room 302." The hotel is a small one, perhaps it's an "**④inn**" or "**⑤hostel**". It's common for people to go to this kind of place when they travel. Whether you travel **⑥domestically** or abroad, you always need a place to stay, which is most likely a hotel. To improve my travel experience, I always choose to stay at an expensive hotel. Also, in order to get a good night's sleep, I'll ask for a quiet room.

中文理解

　　照片裡的人在一家旅館。一位顧客帶著行李箱站在櫃台前。或許她在登記入住，又或許她正在退房。櫃台後面的人是接待員，她正在服務顧客。或許她正在說：「小姐，這是你的房間鑰匙。你的房間是 302。」這間旅館很小，或許是「小旅館」或「旅舍」。人們旅行時常常去這種地方。不管你在國內或者國外旅行，你總是需要住宿的地方，而那最有可能是旅館。為了提升我的旅行體驗，我總是選擇住在昂貴的旅館。還有，為了好好睡一覺，我會要求安靜的房間。

學習解析

❶ suitcase [`sut͵kes] 行李箱 n.

❷ counter [`kaʊntɚ] 櫃台 n.

❸ receptionist [rɪ`sɛpʃənɪst] 接待員 n.

❹ inn [ɪn] 小旅館 n.

❺ hostel [`hɑstl̩] 旅舍（通常指青年旅舍） n.

❻ domestically [də`mɛstɪkl̩ɪ] 在國內 adv.

必殺萬用句

Maybe…, or maybe…

或許…，又或許…

　　其實「看圖敘述」真的很簡單，只有兩個祕訣，第一個是「針對問題回答」，第二個是「在回答的過程中適時使用拖延戰述」。就第一個祕訣而言，如果題目問你「這個人在做什麼？」，你卻只顧著描述他的長相，而完全沒提到他正在做的事，這樣即使你說得再好，也會因為題目問東你說西而無法獲得高分。第二個祕訣則是針對問題回答時，一定要想辦法增加回答的內容。一分半以口說而言並不算短，英語新聞的播報速度大約是每分鐘 120 個單字，所以我們在口說測驗時要想辦法延長回答內容，講難聽一點就是加入「有意義的廢話」，這時候 Maybe..., or maybe... 就是很實用的句型了。

最常考主題
圖片 *11*

Classroom 教室

題目說明

下面有一張圖片及四個相關的問題，請在一分半鐘內完成作答。作答時，請直接回答，不需將題號及題目唸出。

首先請利用 30 秒的時間看圖及問題。

1. 這可能是什麼地方？
2. 圖片中的人在做什麼？
3. 你曾經參與類似的活動嗎？你有什麼感覺？告訴我你的經驗。
4. 如果還有時間，請描述圖片中人物的穿著和景物。

看圖敘述

參考答案

3-11.mp3

The people in the picture are in a classroom. There is a teacher, and there are many students in the classroom. I guess they're elementary school students. I think the teacher is asking some questions, and the students are all raising their hands and trying to give their answers. Wow, these young students are so active in participating❶ in the class, *aren't they?* I guess they're promising❷ students, for they look so enthusiastic❸ about learning. If I were the teacher, I would surely feel satisfied. Of course, I've been a student before, but frankly speaking, I was not so active in answering teachers' questions. I might have been too shy at that age. Now I'm an adult, but the memory of that time is still vivid❹ for me.

中文理解 　　照片裡的人正在教室裡。有一位老師,也有很多學生在教室裡頭。我猜他們是小學生。我想老師正在問一些問題,而所有的學生都舉起手來試圖回答他們的答案。哇,這些年輕的學生很主動參與課堂學習,不是嗎?我猜他們是很有前途的學生,因為他們看起來很熱衷於學習。如果我是那位老師,我一定會感到滿足。當然,我以前當過學生,但坦白說,我不是很主動回答老師的問題。我在那時的年紀可能太害羞了。現在我是個大人了,但那時候的記憶對我來說還是很鮮明。

255

學習解析

❶ participate [pɑr`tɪsə͵pet] 參與 v.

❷ promising [`prɑmɪsɪŋ] 有前途的，前景看好的 adj.

❸ enthusiastic [ɪn͵θjuzɪ`æstɪk] 熱情的 adj.

❹ vivid [`vɪvɪd] 鮮明的 adj.

必殺萬用句

…, aren't they?

…不是嗎？

　　很多國內的考生不是很喜歡用附加問句，這很可能是因為我們在考試時，容易把附加問句歸類為比較「不莊重」的講話方式。當然，外國人在公開演講中很少使用附加問句，但各位不要忘了，「全民英檢」是在測試「日常生活的英語對話能力」。如果你曾經在國外住過一段時間，就會發現外國人使用附加問句的頻率比說中文的我們高出許多。所以，在考試的時候，不妨在適當的時機使用附加問句，這樣才像真正的生活英語，不是嗎？

最常考主題
圖片 *12*

Museum 博物館

題目說明

下面有一張圖片及四個相關的問題,請在一分半鐘內完成作答。作答時,請直接回答,不需將題號及題目唸出。

首先請利用 30 秒的時間看圖及問題。

1. 這可能是什麼地方?
2. 圖片中的人在做什麼?
3. 你曾經去過類似的地方嗎?你為什麼去那裡?告訴我你的經驗。
4. 如果還有時間,請描述圖片中人物的穿著和景物。

參考答案

3-12.mp3

This is an art museum. In the spacious room, there are some paintings hung on the walls. There are a few people appreciating the paintings. I can't see the paintings clearly, but I guess they're portraits or still lifes. Are they created by Picasso, Monnet, or Rembrandt? They're all legendary artists, and I admire them very much. Therefore, I often go to art museums to see their masterpieces. I also try to learn their painting skills, but don't get me wrong. I don't imitate them blindly, and I try to express my own ideas in my works. I believe the sense of aesthetics is key to a quality life, so I encourage people to go to art museums when they have free time.

中文理解

這是一間美術館。在寬敞的房間裡,有一些畫掛在牆上。有幾個人正在欣賞這些畫。我看不清楚那些畫,但我猜它們是肖像畫或靜物畫。它們是畢卡索、莫內或林布蘭創作的嗎?他們都是鼎鼎大名的藝術家,我很崇拜他們。所以,我經常去美術館看他們的傑作。我也試圖學習他們的繪畫技巧,但不要誤會我。我並不是盲目模仿他們,而且我試圖在作品中表達我自己的想法。我相信美感對於高品質的生活很重要,所以我鼓勵人們有空閒的時候就去美術館。

學習解析

❶ spacious [`speʃəs] 寬敞的 adj.

❷ appreciate [ə`priʃɪˌet] 欣賞 v.

❸ portrait [`portret] 肖像畫 n.

❹ still life 靜物畫（複數是 still lifes）

❺ legendary [`lɛdʒəndˌɛrɪ] 名聲顯赫的 adj.

❻ masterpiece [`mæstəˌpis] 傑作 n.

❼ imitate [`ɪməˌtet] 模仿 v.

❽ aesthetics [ɛs`θɛtɪks] 美學 n.

必殺萬用句

This is...

這是…

　　各位看到這樣的句型一定是不會陌生的，早在我們一開始學英語的時候，就常常說 What is this?、This is a book，所以這種句子早就被我們背得滾瓜爛熟了才對。然而，越是簡單的句子，對我們來說才是越可靠的朋友。很多人一到了考場，就因為緊張而把許多平常懂得運用的句型忘了。這時候，別忘了你還有 This is...、That is... 可以用，而且還不太容易用錯呢！

最常考主題
圖片 *13*

Flower Shop 花店

題目說明

下面有一張圖片及四個相關的問題,請在一分半鐘內完成作答。作答時,請直接回答,不需將題號及題目唸出。

首先請利用 30 秒的時間看圖及問題。

1. 這可能是什麼地方?
2. 圖片中的人在做什麼?
3. 你曾經去過類似的地方嗎?告訴我你的經驗。
4. 如果還有時間,請描述圖片中人物的穿著和景物。

參考答案

3-13.mp3

The woman in the picture is in a flower shop. She might be a **florist** at this shop. It seems that many customers have placed their orders, so she's busy dealing with all those flowers. *I see* various kinds of flowers in the picture, *including* roses and **daisies**. They're all so beautiful. I have a lot of experience in buying flowers, so let me talk about it. Before you order flowers, you should definitely compare prices of different shops. You will find that some flower shops sell flowers at lower prices. However, it's also true that higher prices mean better quality, so you'd want to do some **research** on what they can offer. After buying some flowers for yourself, put them somewhere you can easily see. They can help you release your stress, and their **scents** can also cheer you up.

中文理解

照片裡的女子在花店裡。他可能是這間花店的店員。看起來有許多顧客下了訂單,所以她忙著處理這些花。我看見照片裡有各種花,包括玫瑰和雛菊。它們都很美。我有很多買花的經驗,所以讓我談談。在你訂購花之前,你一定該比較不同花店的價格。你會發現有些花用比較低的價格賣花。不過,比較高的價格意味著比較好的品質也是事實,所以你會想要調查一下他們可以提供什麼。為自己買了一些花之後,把它們放在你可以很容易看到的地方。它們可以幫助你釋放壓力,而它們的香味也能讓你開心。

PART 3

學習解析

❶ florist [`flɔrɪst] 花店店員 n.

❷ daisy [`dezɪ] 雛菊 n.

❸ research [`rɪsɝtʃ] 調查 n.

❹ scent [sɛnt] 香味 n.

必殺萬用句

I see…, including…

我看見…，包括…

　　我們看東西的時候，通常會先看整體，然後再分別敘述整體之中的各種事物，這時候 I see..., including... 就是很好用的句型。例如「我看到一些交通標誌，包括停止標誌和禁止左轉標誌」，就可以說成 I see some traffic signs, including a "stop" sign and a "no left turn" sign.。如此一來，除了「交通標誌」這個大單位以外，也可以表達其中的細節，讓你的回答可以多個幾秒。

Lecture Hall　演講廳

題目說明

下面有一張圖片及四個相關的問題,請在一分半鐘內完成作答。作答時,請直接回答,不需將題號及題目唸出。

首先請利用 30 秒的時間看圖及問題。

1. 這可能是什麼地方?
2. 圖片中的人在做什麼?
3. 你曾經去過類似的場合嗎?你有什麼感覺?告訴我你的經驗。
4. 如果還有時間,請描述圖片中人物的穿著和景物。

參考答案

3-14.mp3

A speaker is delivering a speech. The speaker is standing in front of a large audience. ***I'm not sure what*** the ❶occasion is. Maybe they're in class, and the speaker is their teacher, or maybe they're at a ❷seminar or ❸conference. It seems the speaker is so ❹prestigious that a lot of people come to listen to him. I think the picture is taken in a ❺lecture hall. There are two laptop computers in front of the speaker, and he can look at the screens when he forgets his lines. I'm a college student, and I've attended lots of seminars. But I have to say, according to my experience, not everyone can be a ❻professional ❼lecturer. Only those who have fully prepared can deliver a great speech. Next week, I'm going to give a ❽presentation for my term paper in front of my professor and classmates. I hope I can do well.

中文理解

一位演講者正在進行演講。演講者站在一大群聽眾前面。我不確定這是什麼場合。或許他們在上課,而這位演講者是他們的老師,又或者他們是在研討會或者會議中。看起來,這位演講者很有名望,所以很多人來聽他說話。我想這張照片是在演講廳拍的。演講者前面有兩台筆記型電腦,他可以在忘記台詞的時候看螢幕。我是大學生,也參加過許多研討會。但我必須說,根據我的經驗,並不是每個人都能成為專業的演講者。只有完全準備好的人能發表很好的演講。下禮拜,我會為了我的期末報告而在教授和同學前面進行簡報。我希望我能做得好。

學習解析

❶ occasion [əˋkeʒən] 場合 n.

❷ seminar [ˋsɛməˏnɑr] 研討會 n.

❸ conference [ˋkɑnfərəns] 正式的大型會議 n.

❹ prestigious [prɛsˋtɪdʒɪəs] 有名望的 adj.

❺ lecture [ˋlɛktʃə] 授課，演講 n.

❻ professional [prəˋfɛʃənl] 職業性的，專業的 adj.

❼ lecturer [ˋlɛktʃərə] 演講者 n.

❽ presentation [ˏprɛzənˋteʃən] 簡報 n.

必殺萬用句

I'm not sure what...

我不確定…什麼

　　在描述照片的時候，一定會有一些你無法確定的東西，例如照片中人物的感覺，或是一些太小或模糊的東西。就像中文也常說「我不確定這是什麼」、「我不確定那是什麼」一樣，在英語口說測驗中也可以用類似的方式表達。例如 I'm not sure what they're drinking.（我不確定他們在喝什麼）也是一個很典型的例子。只要把 what 後面的內容替換一下，就可以變出許多可以運用的句子了！

最常考主題
圖片 *15*

In The Mountains　在山上

題目說明

下面有一張圖片及四個相關的問題，請在一分半鐘內完成作答。作答時，請直接回答，不需將題號及題目唸出。

首先請利用 30 秒的時間看圖及問題。

1. 這可能是什麼地方？
2. 圖片中的人在做什麼？
3. 你曾經做過類似的活動嗎？你有什麼感覺？告訴我你的經驗。
4. 如果還有時間，請描述圖片中人物的穿著和景物。

3-15.mp3

參考答案

The people in the picture are walking on a **pedestrian suspension bridge**. I also see some **snow-capped** mountains. *I don't know where it is, but* it's **obvious** that the temperature is low, so the mountains must be high. Despite the low temperature, the weather looks nice, and the air seems fresh. Hiking is one of my favorite **recreational activities**. I often go hiking with my friends who have the same hobby. When you're hiking, it's possible that you have to walk across a bridge like this. I admit that sometimes I feel scared when I walk on a suspension bridge because it shakes with every step I take. It may shake even more when the wind is strong. There are many people who refuse to walk on suspension bridges because of **acrophobia**, which means fear of height. However, the view from such bridges is **breathtaking**, so I think they're worth visiting.

中文理解

照片裡的人正在行人吊橋上走路。我也看到一些被雪覆蓋頂部的山。我不知道這是哪裡,但很明顯的是溫度很低,所以這些山一定很高。儘管溫度低,但天氣看起來很好,空氣似乎很新鮮。上山健行是我最愛的休閒活動之一。我常常和有相同嗜好的朋友一起去健行。當你在健行的時候,有可能必須走過像這樣的橋。我承認我走在吊橋上的時候,有時會覺得害怕,因為它會隨著我所走的每一步搖晃。當風很強的時候,可能會搖得更厲害。有很多人拒絕走在吊橋上,因為懼高症的關係,意思就是對高度的恐懼。不過,從這種橋上看到的景色令人嘆為觀止,所以我認為它們值得拜訪。

學習解析

❶ pedestrian suspension bridge 行人吊橋

❷ snow-capped （山）被雪覆蓋頂部的

❸ obvious [`ɑbvɪəs] 明顯的 adj.

❹ recreational activities 休閒活動

❺ acrophobia [ˌækrə`fobɪə] 懼高症 n.

❻ breathtaking [`brɛθˌtekɪŋ] 令人屏息的，美得驚人的 adj.

必殺萬用句

I don't know where it is, but...

我不知道這是哪裡，但⋯

　　英檢中級口說並不是很難，但很多有合格實力的人卻無法通過，問題可能不在於「能力」，而在於「個性」。有些個性比較老實的考生，可能只是題目問什麼就答什麼，而不會用其他的內容來拉長自己的回答時間。例如這句 I don't know where it is，根本就沒有提供什麼資訊，卻增加了回答的長度，不是嗎？

最常考主題
圖片 **16**

On The Street　在街上

題目說明

下面有一張圖片及四個相關的問題，請在一分半鐘內完成作答。作答時，請直接回答，不需將題號及題目唸出。

首先請利用 30 秒的時間看圖及問題。

1. 這可能是什麼地方？
2. 圖片中的人在做什麼？
3. 你曾經看過類似的活動嗎？告訴我你的經驗。
4. 如果還有時間，請描述圖片中人物的穿著和景物。

參考答案

3-16.mp3

It seems that the picture was taken by a **canal**❶ in a foreign country. There is a bridge on the canal. The people standing by the canal are **street performers**❷. They're a band of five or six musicians. I see a man playing the **saxophone**❸, a man playing the trumpet, and another playing the **keyboard**❹. There is also a drum, but I'm not sure if someone is playing it. There is also a saxophone case on the ground. *That's all I see in the picture.* In Taiwan, we can find some street performers in the **vicinity**❺ of major tourist **attractions**❻. I think they're all **talented**❼, and they're **devoted**❽ to their performance, just like stage performers do. Oh, I remember once I saw a wonderful performance near my school, and I gave the performers two hundred dollars. I believe we should pay for their performance if we enjoy it. What do you think about it?

中文理解　　看起來這張照片是在國外的一座運河旁邊拍的。運河上有一座橋。站在運河旁邊的人是街頭藝人。他們是五或六位樂手組成的樂團。我看見一個演奏薩克斯風的男人，一個演奏小號的男人，還有一個是演奏鍵盤的。還有一個鼓，但我不確定是否有人在打鼓。地上也有一個裝薩克斯風的盒子。我在照片裡看到的就是這些。在台灣，我們可以在主要觀光景點附近發現一些街頭藝人。我認為他們都很有才華，而且他們投入於自己的表演，就像舞台藝人一樣。噢，我記得有一次在學校附近看到很棒的表演，而我給了那些表演者兩百元。我相信如果我們享受他們的表演，就應該為表演付費。你認為呢？

學習解析

❶ canal [kə`næl] 運河 n.

❷ street performer 街頭藝人（表演者）

❸ saxophone [`sæksə͵fon] 薩克斯風 n.

❹ keyboard [`ki͵bord] 鍵盤 n.

❺ vicinity [və`sɪnətɪ] 鄰近地區 n.

❻ attraction [ə`trækʃən] 景點 n.

❼ talented [`tæləntɪd] 有才華的 adj.

❽ devoted [dɪ`votɪd] 投入的 adj.

必殺萬用句

That's all I see in the picture.

我在照片裡看到的就是這些。

　　有時候，看圖敘述的照片不會有太多細節，如果只是敘述照片上的東西，恐怕很快就無話可說了。所以，除了照片中的內容以外，也需要說明自己有過的類似經驗，能把這兩部分做好，就是很完整的回答了。當照片內容的敘述告一段落，想要開始談自己的經驗時，就可以說 That's all I see in the picture.，表示照片中內容已經沒什麼可以談的了，接下來就可以延伸討論相關的事情。

Chapter 3
模擬試題

中級口說測驗
一回完整模擬
試題 & 解答

全民英語能力分級檢定測驗

中級口說能力測驗

test.mp3

請在 15 秒以內完成並唸出下列自我介紹的句子：

My seat number is （座位號碼後 5 碼）, and my registration number is （考試號碼後 5 碼）.

第一部分：朗讀短文

　　請先利用 1 分鐘的時間閱讀下面的短文，然後在 2 分鐘內以正常的速度，清楚正確的讀出下面的短文，閱讀時請不要發出聲音。

　　All schools will be closed today due to heavy rain last night. Some parts of the city are still flooded, so all students are advised to stay at home. While a few schools decided to move instruction online, others choose to dismiss classes today. Flash flood warnings have been in effect since Wednesday evening in some areas, and another storm system is expected to bring heavy rainfall again this weekend, so please stay tuned for the latest weather updates.

＊　　　　　　＊　　　　　　＊

　　Enjoy the full use of our facilities when you stay at Dynasty Hotel. Located on the first floor is our coffee shop, where you can enjoy light meals and beverages. On the 11th floor, there is a French restaurant offering three-course meals. Prices start from $19.99. To make a reservation, please call 128-9074. For those who enjoy working out, our gym is on the 3rd floor, open from 9:00 A.M. to 10:00 P.M. every day except Wednesday.

第二部分：回答問題

　　這個部分共有 10 題，題目已事先錄音，每題經由耳機播出二次，不印在試卷上。第 1 至 5 題，每題回答時間 15 秒；第 6 至 10 題，每題回答時間 30 秒。每題播出後，請立即回答。回答時，不一定要用完整的句子，但請在作答時間內儘量的表達。

第三部分：看圖敘述

　　下面有一張圖片及四個相關的問題，請在一分半鐘內完成作答。作答時，請直接回答，不需將題號及題目唸出。

　　首先請利用 30 秒的時間看圖及問題。

1. 這可能是什麼地方？你怎麼知道？
2. 圖片中的人在做什麼？
3. 你曾經做過類似的事嗎？告訴我你的經驗。
4. 如果還有時間，請描述圖片中人物的穿著和景物。

請將下列自我介紹的句子再唸一遍：

My seat number is （座位號碼後 5 碼）, and my registration number is （考試號碼後 5 碼）.

Part 1 朗讀短文

test-a1.mp3

(發音提示) 粗體套色字為重音，加底線者為連音。

All schools will be **closed today** due to **heavy rain last night.**
Some parts of the **city** are still **flooded**❶, so **all students** are advised to
stay at home. While a **few schools** decided to **move instruction**❷
online, **others** choose to **dismiss classes today**❸. **Flash flood**❹
warnings have been in **effect** since **Wednesday evening** in some areas,
and **another storm system** is expected to bring **heavy rainfall again**❺
this **weekend**, so **please stay tuned**❻ for the **latest weather updates**.

中文理解　　由於昨晚的大雨，所有學校今天都將關閉。本市部
分地區仍然淹水，所以建議所有學生留在家中。雖然有
幾所學校決定改為線上教學，但其他學校選擇今天不上課。從週三晚間開始，部
分地區就已經發布了洪水警報，而本週末預計另一個風暴系統將再度帶來大量降
雨，所以請不要轉台，以獲得最新氣象資訊。

學習解析

❶ flood [flʌd] 淹沒，使淹水 v.

❷ instruction [ɪn`strʌkʃən] 教學 n.

❸ dismiss [dɪs`mɪs] 不予考慮，解散 v.

❹ flash flood 突然發生的水災

❺ rainfall [`ren͵fɔl] 降雨 n.

❻ stay tuned 鎖定頻道不轉台

(發音提示) 粗體套色字為重音，加底線者為連音。

Enjoy the **full use** of our **facilities** when you **stay** at **Dynasty Hotel**. **Located** on the **first floor** is our **coffee shop**, where you can enjoy **light meals** and **beverages**. On the **eleventh floor**, there is a **French restaurant** offering **three-course meals**. **Prices** start from **$19.99**. To make a **reservation**, **please call 128-9074**. For those who enjoy **working out**, our **gym** is on the **third floor**, open from **nine A.M.** to **ten P.M.** every day except Wednesday.

*「$19.99」可以唸成 nineteen dollars and ninety-nine cents，或者採用日常生活中的簡化說法 nineteen ninety-nine（不說出 dollar 和 cent）。電話號碼中的「0」可以唸成 zero 或「oh」。

在朝代飯店住宿時，請盡情使用我們的設施。位於一樓的是我們的咖啡店，您可以在那裡享受輕食和飲料。在十一樓，有一間提供三道料理式全餐的法式餐廳。價格從 19.99 美元起。如需預約，請撥 128-9074。對於喜愛運動的人，我們的健身房在三樓，除了星期三以外，每天上午 9:00 至晚上 10:00 開放。

學習解析

❶ facility [fə`sɪlətɪ] 設施 n.

❷ dynasty [`daɪnəstɪ] 朝代 n.

❸ located [`loketɪd] 位於某處的 adj.

❹ beverage [`bɛvərɪdʒ] 飲料 n.

❺ reservation [ˌrɛzəˋveʃən] 預約 n.

答題示範

Part 2 回答問題

 test-a2.mp3

1 ## Do you usually eat dinner at home? Why or why not?

你通常在家中吃晚餐嗎？為什麼？

參考答案

I don't eat dinner at home very often because I usually work^❶ overtime and eat takeout^❷ food in my office. Therefore, I make it a rule^❸ to have dinner with my family on weekends so we can spend some time together.

我不是很常在家吃晚餐，因為我通常會加班並且在辦公室吃外帶的食物。所以，我習慣在週末和我的家人吃晚餐，好讓我們可以共同度過一些時間。

學習解析

❶ work overtime 加班工作（工作超過下班時間）

❷ takeout [`tek͵aʊt] （食物）外帶的 adj.

❸ make it a rule to do 習慣做…

Do you like to listen to music in your free time? What kind of music do you like?

你喜歡在空閒時刻聽音樂嗎？你喜歡什麼類型的音樂？

Yes, in my leisure time❶, I always listen to music. I think my favorite genre❷ is jazz. Every time I listen to jazz music, I feel relaxed❸ and calm. Actually, I also listen to jazz when I work, and I'm more productive❹ with music on.

是的，在我的休閒時間，我總是聽音樂。我想我最愛的類型是爵士。每當我聽爵士音樂的時候，我覺得放鬆又平靜。事實上，我工作時也聽爵士，而且我開著音樂的時候比較有生產力。

學習解析

❶ leisure time 休閒時間
❷ genre [ˋʒɑnrə]（音樂、文藝作品的）類型 n.
❸ relaxed [rɪˋlækst] 感到放鬆的 adj.
❹ productive [prəˋdʌktɪv] 有生產力的 adj.

Have you ever cheated on an exam? What do you think about cheating?

你曾經在考試作弊嗎？你對於作弊的想法是什麼？

To be honest, I've cheated❶ on exams several times before. I did that because my classmates asked me to cheat with them, and I didn't want to be the odd one out❷. I felt guilty❸ because it's like lying to my teachers.

老實說，我以前曾經在考試作弊過幾次。我那麼做是因為同學要我跟他們一起作弊，而我不想當個異類。我覺得有罪惡感，因為那就像是對老師說謊一樣。

學習解析

❶ cheat [tʃit] 作弊 v.

❷ the odd one out 異類，不合群的人

❸ guilty [`ɡɪltɪ] 有罪的，有罪惡感的 adj.

④ Your cousin Patricia works as a fashion designer. Ask her some questions about her job.

你的表姊派翠西亞是一位時尚設計師。問她一些有關她工作的問題。

Hi, sis. I know you have a good fashion sense, and you're good at ❶ sketching, but I'm always ❷ curious where your ❸ inspiration comes from. What's the ❹ concept behind your latest works? Do you watch fashion shows to get ideas for new designs?

嗨，姊。我知道你對時尚很有敏感度，也擅長速寫（素描），但我總是好奇你的靈感來自哪裡。你最新作品背後的概念是什麼？你會看時裝秀來獲得新設計的想法嗎？

學習解析

❶ sketch [skɛtʃ] 速寫（素描）v.

❷ curious [`kjʊrɪəs] 好奇的 adj.

❸ inspiration [ˌɪnspə`reʃən] 靈感 n.

❹ concept [`kɑnsɛpt] 概念 n.

5 Your friend Owen wants to quit his current job and find a new one. Give him some advice.

你的朋友歐文想要辭去他現在的工作並且找新的。給他一些建議。

 Owen, I heard that you want to change jobs, but in my opinion, I won't say it's a good decision during this time of recession. You know what? It's really hard to find a new job, whether full-time or part-time, so keep your current job, or you'll regret it.

歐文，我聽說你想要換工作，但就我來看，我不會說在這個經濟衰退的時候是個好的決定。你知道嗎？找到新的工作真的很難，不管是全職還是兼職，所以保留你現在的工作吧，不然你會後悔的。

學習解析

❶ recession [rɪ`sɛʃən]（經濟的）衰退 n.

❷ regret [rɪ`grɛt] 後悔 v.

6 How do you usually celebrate Mother's Day? Tell me about your experience.

你通常怎麼慶祝母親節？告訴我你的經驗。

My mother likes Japanese food, so my family and I usually go to a nice Japanese restaurant to celebrate Mother's Day. If the restaurant allows, we'll also bring a cake to make the day more **memorable**[1]. After eating **to our hearts' content**[2], we'll go to a **karaoke**[3]. My mother loves singing, and she feels happy when we **applaud**[4] her **performance**[5]. It also makes us happy to see her **enjoying herself**[6].

我的母親喜歡日式料理，所以我的家人和我通常會去很好的日式餐廳慶祝母親節。如果餐廳允許的話，我們也會帶蛋糕，讓這一天更難忘。吃得心滿意足之後，我們會去卡拉 OK。我的母親喜愛唱歌，當我們對她的表演鼓掌時，她會覺得高興。看到她過得愉快，也會讓我們很高興。

學習解析

❶ memorable [`mɛmərəbl] 值得紀念的 adj.

❷ to one's heart's content 盡情地

❸ karaoke [ˌkɑrɑ`oke] 卡拉 OK，KTV n.

❹ applaud [ə`plɔd] 鼓掌 v.

❺ performance [pə`fɔrməns] 表演 n.

❻ enjoy oneself 過得愉快

7 Do you know anyone who can speak English pretty well? What might be the reason that they are so fluent?

你認識英語說得很不錯的人嗎？他們這麼流利的原因可能是什麼？

My cousin hasn't studied abroad, yet she can speak English just like a native speaker does. She once told me that she used to attend English courses at a language school to practice conversation. She worked very hard and took every chance to communicate in English. That's why she can speak English so fluently. The more we use a language, the more our language skills will grow.

我的堂姊不曾出國留學，卻能把英語講得像母語人士一樣。她曾經告訴我，她以前經常上語言補習班的英語課程來練習會話。她很努力，並且把握每個用英語溝通的機會。那就是她能把英語說得這麼流利的原因。我們越常使用一種語言，我們的語言能力就會成長越多。

學習解析

❶ native speaker 母語人士

❷ language school 語言補習班

❸ communicate [kə`mjunə͵ket] 溝通 v.

❹ fluently [`fluəntlɪ] 流利地 adv.

8 If you could travel to Mars, what would you do there?

如果你能前往火星，你會在那裡做什麼？

Go to **Mars**❶? I'm interested in it! Well, if I could fly to Mars, I'd like to find out if there are **aliens**❷ living on that **gorgeous**❸ planet. I want to know how they live their lives, and how they communicate with each other. I'd also like to **investigate**❹ whether there are animals or plants on the planet. It would be interesting to know the differences between **creatures**❺ on Mars and those on the Earth.

去火星嗎？我有興趣！嗯，假如我可以飛到火星，我想看看是否有外星人住在那個美麗的星球。我想要知道他們如何生活，以及他們是怎麼和彼此溝通的。我也想調查那個星球上是否有動物或植物。知道火星生物和地球生物的差異會是很有趣的。

學習解析

❶ Mars [mɑrz] 火星 n.

❷ alien [`elɪən] 外星人 n.

❸ gorgeous [`gɔrdʒəs] 非常漂亮的 adj.

❹ investigate [ɪn`vɛstə͵get] 調查 v.

❺ creature [`kritʃɚ] 生物 n.

9 What are some advantages or disadvantages of getting a flu vaccine?

打流感疫苗的好處或壞處是什麼？

When the flu season is approaching❶, getting a flu vaccine❷ becomes a hot issue. In my opinion, vaccination❸ is an effective way to reduce chances of getting the flu, so I get vaccinated❹ every year. However, some people choose not to get vaccinated because they're afraid of possible side effects❺, such as allergies❻. Well, every coin has two sides❼, so I respect their choice.

當流感季節接近時，接種流感疫苗就成為熱門的議題。就我看來，疫苗接種是減少得流感機率的有效方法，所以我每年都接種疫苗。不過，有些人選擇不接種疫苗，因為他們害怕可能的副作用，例如過敏。嗯，每件事都是一體兩面，所以我尊重他們的選擇。

學習解析

❶ approach [ə`protʃ] 接近 v.

❷ vaccine [`væksin] 疫苗 n.

❸ vaccination [ˌvæksən`eʃən] 疫苗接種 n.

❹ vaccinate [`væksənˌet] 為…注射疫苗 v.

❺ side effect 副作用

❻ allergy [`æləˌdʒɪ] 過敏 n.

❼ every coin has two sides 每個硬幣都有兩面；每件事都是一體兩面

10 Are you satisfied with your physical appearance? Why or why not?

你對自己的身體外貌（包括臉和身材）滿意嗎？為什麼？

 To tell the truth, I'm not satisfied with my **body shape**①. I'm **overweight**② and not tall, so some of my classmates call me "piggy". I really hate this **nickname**③. I don't expect myself to become as tall and thin as a model one day, but I do believe I can lose some weight and look like an **average**④ woman if I work hard. Therefore, I make it a rule to exercise every day, and I avoid eating things after 9 P.M. I hope that will work!

說實話，我不滿意自己的體型。我過重而且不高，所以有些同學叫我「小豬」。我真的很討厭這個綽號。我不期望自己有一天變得像模特兒一樣又高又瘦，但我相信如果我努力的話，我可以減掉一些體重，並且看起來像是一般的女性。所以，我固定每天做運動，也避免在晚上 9 點之後吃東西。我希望會有效！

學習解析

① body shape 體型
② overweight [`ovəˌwet] 過重的 adj.
③ nickname [`nɪkˌnem] 綽號 n.
④ average [`ævərɪdʒ] 平均的，一般的 adj.

Part 3 看圖敘述

 test-a3.mp3

1. 這可能是什麼地方？你怎麼知道？
2. 圖片中的人在做什麼？
3. 你曾經做過類似的事嗎？告訴我你的經驗。
4. 如果還有時間，請描述圖片中人物的穿著和景物。

參考答案

The sign says "Taipei Station", and it's quite **spacious** ❶ here, so I think it's the **lobby** ❷ of the railway station. There's a huge **timetable** ❸ on the top of the picture, showing what time each train will arrive. Below the timetable are the station's service counters. There are quite a few people waiting in line to get their tickets. I often take a train to my **hometown** ❹ in the south of Taiwan, and I always **book** ❺ my ticket **in advance** ❻. However, I do it online instead of going to the station. It's convenient to book online, but it's still difficult to get tickets for holidays such as Chinese New Year, Dragon Boat Festival, and Mid-Autumn Festival. That's because many people go back to their hometowns by train during these holidays, yet the seats are limited. You have to log on to the booking website as soon as the tickets go on sale, or you'll end up without a seat. It's a lot of trouble, and I don't think the **situation** ❼ will improve anytime soon.

　　看板上寫著「台北車站」，而且這裡很寬敞，所以我認為這是鐵路車站的大廳。照片上方有個很大的時刻表，顯示每輛列車幾點會到站。時間表下面是車站的服務櫃台。有不少人為了買票而正在排隊。我常常搭火車到我在台灣南部的家鄉，而且我總是事先訂購我的車票。不過，我是在網路上訂票，而不是去車站。在網路上訂票很方便，但要買到農曆新年、端午節、中秋節之類假日的車票還是很難。這是因為有很多人會在這些假期搭火車回到他們的家鄉，但座位卻有限。你必須在車票一開賣的時候就上訂票網站，不然你就會沒有座位。這很麻煩，我也不認為這個狀況會在短期之內改善。

學習解析

❶ spacious [`speʃəs] 寬敞的 adj.

❷ lobby [`lɑbɪ] 大廳 n.

❸ timetable [`taɪmˌtebl] 時刻表 n.

❹ hometown [`hom`taʊn] 故鄉，家鄉 n.

❺ book [bʊk] 預訂 v.

❻ in advance 事先，預先

❼ situation [ˌsɪtʃʊ`eʃən] 狀況 n.

國際學村　LA PRESS 語研學院 Language Academy Press

語言學習NO.1

學英語

English Stylebook
英文寫作的法則

拆字規則、標點符號、特殊符號、文體寫作 石井隆之／著

教你寫出與英語母語人士相同的
商用英文、電子郵件、私函格式、學術論文、英文格式書
以防止令人尷尬、令人誤解的英語寫作技巧與知識

學韓語

一掃你的學習障礙

韓語文法
精準剖析

第一線教育專家歸納！
必學生活各種主題教學，韓語母語學習一次學會！
強力推薦
韓語佐藤／首爾大學韓語教育學科文學碩士 楊人鉉教授

學日語

一看就懂的
日語文法入門書

我的第一本
日語文法

本書適用完全初學、從零開始的日語文法學習者！

JAPANESE
Grammar in use！

Beginning to Early Intermediate

五十嵐幸子／著

第二外語

實境式

全系列1500個實境圖解

照片單字全部收錄

圖解德語單字 不用背

一眼秒懂德文單字、理解當地文化

侯秀琳／著

德國／奧地利留學工面試嗎？還有哪些準備？

（德語單字表格插圖）

本書適用德語「初級～中、高級」階段，專為只想學單字的你準備！

QR碼線上音檔、隨刷隨聽

考多益

HACKERS × 國際學村

新制多益
全新！TOEIC
閱讀題庫解析
Reading

Hackers Academia、張秉洙·Tina／著

每月進場實測分析、完整傳授解題技巧
黃金證書手到擒來！

全新收錄
精準10回
模擬試題

考日檢

新日檢
JLPT N3

新日檢滿點！

合格模試

3回模擬試題

令和最新版

全新仿真模考題！
含逐題完整解析，滿分不是夢！

考韓檢

New
TOPIK II

新韓檢
寫作應考
祕笈

中高級

獨家授權繁體中文版

考英檢

NEW
GEPT
新制全民英檢

符合110年更新題型
聽力測驗MP3+QR碼線上音檔

10回試題完全掌握最新內容與趨勢！

初級

聽力&閱讀
題庫大全

想獲得最新最快的
語言學習情報嗎？

歡迎加入
國際學村&語研學院粉絲團

台灣廣廈 國際出版集團
Taiwan Mansion International Group

國家圖書館出版品預行編目（CIP）資料

新制全民英檢中級口說測驗必考題型／陳頎著.
-- 初版. -- 新北市：國際學村，2021.10
　　面；　公分
ISBN 978-986-454-179-9（平裝）
1.英語　2.能力測驗

805.1892　　　　　　　　　　110013802

國際學村

NEW GEPT 新制全民英檢中級口說測驗必考題型
從發音基礎、答題策略到解題示範，自學、初學者也能循序漸進獲得高分！

作　　　者／陳頎　　　　　　　　編輯中心編輯長／伍峻宏・編輯／賴敬宗
監　　　修／國際語言中心委員會　封面設計／何偉凱・內頁排版／菩薩蠻數位文化有限公司
　　　　　　　　　　　　　　　　製版・印刷・裝訂／皇甫・秉成

行企研發中心總監／陳冠蒨　　　媒體公關組／陳柔彣
　　　　　　　　　　　　　　　綜合業務組／何欣穎

發　行　人／江媛珍
法 律 顧 問／第一國際法律事務所 余淑杏律師・北辰著作權事務所 蕭雄淋律師
出　　　版／國際學村
發　　　行／台灣廣廈有聲圖書有限公司
　　　　　　地址：新北市235中和區中山路二段359巷7號2樓
　　　　　　電話：（886）2-2225-5777・傳真：（886）2-2225-8052

代理印務・全球總經銷／知遠文化事業有限公司
　　　　　　地址：新北市222深坑區北深路三段155巷25號5樓
　　　　　　電話：（886）2-2664-8800・傳真：（886）2-2664-8801
郵 政 劃 撥／劃撥帳號：18836722
　　　　　　劃撥戶名：知遠文化事業有限公司（※單次購書金額未滿1000元需另付郵資70元。）

■出版日期：2021年10月
ISBN：978-986-454-179-9　　　版權所有，未經同意不得重製、轉載、翻印。

Complete Copyright © 2021 by Taiwan Mansion Publishing Co., Ltd.
All rights reserved.